# A DEATH

*Notes of a Suicide*

ZALMAN SHNEOUR

*translated by Daniel Kennedy*

WAKEFIELD PRESS

CAMBRIDGE, MASSACHUSETTS

Wakefield Press, P.O. Box 425645, Cambridge, MA 02142

Originally published as *A Toyt: Shriftn fun a zelbstmerder a tiref* in 1909.

Cover image: Frans Masereel, "The City/Die Stadt" © 2019 Artists Rights Society (ARS), New York / VG Bild-Kunst, Bonn
Frontispiece: The Jewish quarter of Prague, demolished sometime between 1893 and 1913.

This book was set in Garamond Premier Pro and Helvetica Neue Pro by Wakefield Press. Printed and bound by McNaughton & Gunn, Inc., in the United States of America.

ISBN: 978-1-939663-45-0

Available through D.A.P./Distributed Art Publishers
75 Broad Street, Suite 630
New York, New York 10004
Tel: (212) 627-1999
Fax: (212) 627-9484

1   2   3   4   5   6   7   8   9   10

# A DEATH

# CONTENTS

# TRANSLATOR'S INTRODUCTION

> *The Thought of Death.*—It gives me a melancholy happiness to live in the midst of this confusion of streets, of necessities, of voices: how much enjoyment, impatience and desire, how much thirsty life and drunkenness of life comes to light here every moment! And yet it will soon be so still for all these shouting, lively, life-loving people!
>
> > Friedrich Nietzsche, *The Joyful Wisdom*, trans. Thomas Common

> "Friends," cried Zverkov, getting up from the sofa. "Let us all be off now, *there*!"
>
> > Fyodor Dostoevsky, *Notes from Underground*, trans. Constance Garnett

For the Jews of Eastern Europe at the turn of the nineteenth century, the act of writing in one's mother tongue was neither an unremarkable nor an obvious choice. Yiddish was widely spoken throughout the Russian and Austro-Hungarian empires, the vernacular of the overwhelming majority of Ashkenazi Jewry, yet it was discriminated against not just by the outside world, but also internally. Traditional Jewish literacy was centered around the learning of the liturgical tongues: Hebrew and, to a lesser extent, Aramaic. While European literature was still dominated by literary super-powers—French, English, German, and Russian—the nineteenth century brought a flourishing of minor literatures nourished by the awakening of national consciousness.

Nineteenth-century Jewish literature was dominated by the *Haskole* movement, or so-called Jewish Enlightenment. *Maskilim* (proponents of the Haskole) had the twofold mission of transforming Hebrew from the liturgical language of religious practice into a full-fledged modern literary language, and fostering the notion of a secular Jewish education in an effort to combat what they saw as widespread dogma and superstition. The Hebrew language once again became a vehicle for contemporary scientific, philosophical, and poetic ideas, but the potential audience for such a literature remained small owing to the fact that most Jews had limited literacy in Hebrew. Reluctantly at first, the Maskilim soon began producing material in the vernacular of the Jewish masses: Yiddish.

By the turn of the twentieth century, writers such as Isaac Meyer Dik (1807–1893) and Mendele Moykher Sforim (1836–1917) had succeeded in transforming Yiddish from a didactic vehicle, aimed predominantly at women and uneducated men, into a popular and sophisticated medium for literary expression. And so, dwarfed by neighboring giants German and Russian, the two fledgling literatures grew up side by side, occupying the same geographical space, jostling for the same readership, and often flowing from the very same pens. Both languages were in a state of flux: Hebrew was in the process of being rebuilt from the ground up, while for Yiddish the literary standard language was beginning to solidify, comprising elements of the various spoken dialects.

◆

Zalman (Zalkind) Shneour was born in 1887 in Shklow (modern-day Belarus, then part of the Russian Empire), the fourth of seven children, into a middle-class Hasidic Jewish family related to the Shneerson rabbinical dynasty.

His father, a merchant dealing in antiques and precious stones, spent nine months a year traveling between Moscow and Warsaw, buying and selling merchandise.[1]

Shneour received a strict traditional religious education up to the age of eleven. His father was an avid reader of Kabbalah and would feed his children's imagination by recounting Hasidic wonder-tales and Torah stories, emphasizing the mystical elements. When Shneour was later exposed to secular subjects such as Russian and Modern Hebrew, his interest in literature blossomed and he began devouring Hebrew poetry with an insatiable appetite. By the age of eight he had begun writing his own poems in Hebrew and Yiddish. His passion for literature soon brought the young Zalman into conflict with his father, who wanted him to go into commerce. Zalman persisted, and when he was twelve his father took him to Warsaw to meet with Nahum Sokolow (1859–1936), editor-in-chief of the Hebrew daily newspaper *Ha-Tsefirah*, to discuss the feasibility of Zalman becoming a writer. Nothing came of the meeting and the Shneours returned home, neither having managed to change the other's mind.[2]

A year later, no longer able to stand the atmosphere of his childhood home, Zalman ran away to Odessa—a city home to a vibrant Hebrew literary scene—where he was welcomed by preeminent poet Hayim Nahman Bialik (1873–1934), and made the acquaintance of the likes of Mendele, Yehoshua Ravnitski (1859–1944), and Simon Dubnow (1860–1941). Shneour enrolled in university, but without financial support from home he lived in extreme poverty and was eventually forced to suspend his studies and move to Warsaw where he secured a job in the newly formed Tushiya publishing house, the first privately owned modern Jewish secular press.[3] In Warsaw he began to publish his first literary works, starting with Hebrew poetry in the children's magazine *Olam Katan*, and Yiddish Poetry in the *Yidishe folkstsaytung*.[4] In 1902, growing tired of menial work at Tushiya, he resigned and, after a brief stint as personal secretary to Yiddish writer (and de facto patriarch of Warsaw's Yiddish literary circle) I. L. Peretz (1852–1915), secured a position on the staff of the prestigious Hebrew literary magazine *Ha-Dor*, where his new boss and mentor David Frishman (1859–1922) taught him everything he needed to know about the business side of literature. Shneour kept a foot in both camps, joining the Hebraist circle of Fishman, while continuing to frequent the Yiddish literary circle around Peretz.

Meanwhile, Shneour's literary horizons began to expand. In addition to making a name for himself as a promising Hebrew poet (Bialik would later hail him as one of the great new poets: "Here is Shneour—a young 'Samson' who overnight grew all seven of his tresses"),[5] Shneour also began writing short stories and comical sketches in both languages, as well as Yiddish poems, which would later become immortalized as popular folk songs.[6]

◆

The year 1904 saw the opening of *Ha-Zeman*, a new Hebrew language daily newspaper in Vilna (modern-day Vilnius, Lithuania). Many Litvaks[7] who had found employment in the Warsaw publishing world, Shneour among them, saw this as an opportunity to earn a living closer to home.

Shneour lived in Vilne from 1904 to 1906 during a period of unprecedented political turmoil in the Russian Empire; beginning with the Russo-Japanese war and culminating in the failed revolution of 1905 and its aftermath, it was a time of widespread instability, riots, labor-stoppages, anti-Jewish pogroms, and political assassinations.

There Shneour fell in with a circle of like-minded young Jewish writers and intellectuals, which included Peretz Hirshbeyn (1880–1948), Yitskhak Dov Berkowitz (1885–1967), Ernestina Rabinowitz (1884–1938), and Y. Bershadsky (1871–1908). Eighteen years old, Shneour was the baby of the group. His hair, which he had previously worn long in the style of an Orthodox priest, was now cut short, and he began to dress in the dandyish fashion of his peers. His new roommate Berkowitz, who had befriended Shneour in Warsaw, described the enthusiasm with which Shneour came to Vilna:

> Shneour was a young, slender, and energetic transplant to our new Vilna colony. His Litvak heart could no longer resist the call: no sooner had I described in my letters to him the charms of the city than he abandoned Warsaw, paid a visit to his native Shklow for passover, and came to settle in the reborn "Jerusalem of the North."[8]

One thing that set this group apart from similar groups in Warsaw or Odessa—where the first walls would soon be erected between the hitherto porous worlds of Yiddish and Hebrew letters—was their commitment to the idea of Jewish bilingualism and passion for self-translation (though this passion was not purely ideological or aesthetic: dire economic conditions meant that they needed wares to sell, and Yiddish was a significantly more lucrative commodity than Hebrew). Bershadsky, the elder of the group, who in 1905 would be forced to retire from editing *Ha-Zeman* owing to tuberculosis, proposed a unique plan: to become a single association, with the aim of translating their own works.[9] It was in this context that Shneour took one of his Hebrew short stories written three years earlier, "Min ha-Mavet," and translated, adapted, and expanded it into the full length Yiddish novella, *A toyt: Shriftn fun a zelbsmerder a tiref*.[10]

The plan was prescient, as the post-1905 easing of strict Tsarist press controls led to a proliferation of new Yiddish language newspapers and with them opportunities to publish. Soon Shneour's first books began to come out—notably, a Hebrew poetry collection and a book of Hebrew children's stories—culminating in 1909 with the release of four books: his collected Yiddish short stories, a collection of Yiddish poems, and the Yiddish version and a new Hebrew translation of *A Death*.

◆

*A Death* had as its backdrop a large, unnamed Eastern European city. This dark, expressionist cityscape, lacking discernible landmarks or identifying features, full of bustling streets and constant noise, is contrasted with the protagonist's hometown, a distant provincial market town. The novella takes the form of a diary as a narrative device, granting the reader access to the protagonist's inner world—a world filled with demons, both figurative and hallucinated; where ideas feed and grow inside you like parasites; where shadows dance on the walls to the tune of the characters' moods. It is a world home to perhaps the most singular supporting character in all of Yiddish literature: a hungry, spiteful, sensually charged revolver.

The diary follows the Jewish calendar, beginning during the month of Elel (Heb. *Elul*), the traditional month of introspection and soul-searching, spanning the High Holidays and the Autumnal festival of Sukkes.

The narrator, Shloyme (or Salomon, as he is known to his semi-assimilated Russian-Speaking acquaintances), is a variant of a stock character popular in Jewish literature of the day—shaped by the likes of Hersh Dovid Nomberg (1876–1927), Berkovitsh, and Chaim Brenner (1881–1921)—known in Hebrew as a *talush* (lit.: "uprooted one"), and in Yiddish as a *Fliglman* (after the protagonist of Nomberg's eponymous short story). A typical Fliglman is a young man who has left the provinces, leaving behind his family, religious faith, and traditional lifestyle to broaden his intellectual horizons (usually involving an excessive consumption of Spinoza, Schopenhauer, and Nietzsche) and explore a new, modern life in the big city—only to find spiritual disaffection, economic instability, social isolation, and a chronic inability to relate to women.[11] But Shloyme is a self-aware Fliglman, and, recognizing in himself the traits of this stereotype, is filled with violent self-loathing:

TRANSLATOR'S INTRODUCTION

I know the type. They emerge from the *yeshivas* and from dark corners of their small-town parents' houses, seeking a "*goal.*" They set off for the big cities, starve and languish in cellars, begging and earning a pittance from private lessons. They in turn take lessons from other students for next to nothing. Their brief youths stifled among dusty books, of no use to anyone. And by the time they've attained their goals they are already sick, depressed, and broken for good. Consumptive, short-sighted, emaciated, with protruding Adam's apples. I can't stand those sickly, talentless scholars with their pure diplomas, with their sunken chests, without flesh, without life. I can't stand those victims of education.

This subgenre of Jewish literature, exploring the lives of characters on the margins of Jewish society—characters bearing striking biographical similarities to many Jewish writers themselves—borrowed stylistically and thematically from Russian literature, particularly Dostoevsky. *A Death* calls explicit attention to this influence with allusions to Dostoevsky's *Notes from Underground*, specifically in its repetition of the euphemistic phrasing characters use when speaking of visiting a brothel: *tuda/ahin* (italicized in both) meaning *there* (in the sense of "to there/thither"). Shneour drew further attention to this intertextuality when he reprinted the book in 1923 by changing the title from *a toyt* ("A Death") to *ahin* ("There").

Shneour was far from the first Yiddish writer to critique the restrictive nature of traditional Jewish society, but he was unsurpassed in his ability to articulate the seething resentment of those who did not fit in. While his later works would explore this same alienation with more breadth and nuance, *A Death* captures this rage and suffocating desperation with energy and originality.

◆

Shneour went on to travel extensively throughout Western Europe, notably Switzerland, France (where he studied medicine), and Germany. He spent the First World War in a German prison on account of his Russian citizenship.

By the mid-1920s, the two strands of Jewish literature had gone their separate paths. Palestine had become the definitive epicenter of Hebrew publishing, while Yiddish publishing was concentrated mostly in the newly independent Poland and the United States. Shneour, now based permanently in Paris, attempted to work in both markets but was significantly more successful in Yiddish and soon he began writing prose exclusively in that language. Throughout the 1920s and early 1930s he enjoyed critical, popular, and financial success with his *Shklover yidn (Jews of Shklow)* cycle, a series of short stories, set in his hometown. The stories—over a hundred in all—were published weekly in both the *Moment* (Warsaw) and *Forverts* (New York), and were followed by various book-length collections. Ranging from the nostalgic to the satirical, they were praised for their humor and sharply tuned psychological insight. Other major works included *Noyekh Pandre* (Noah Pandre), a picaresque epic in five volumes, and *Keyser un rebe* (The emperor and the rabbi), a sprawling multivolume historical novel centered around the figures of Napoleon and the Lubavitcher Rabbi, Shneour Zalman Schneersohn (Shneour's aforementioned famous ancestor). Other stand-alone novels included *A tog oylem haze* (A day of worldly pleasures), *Di meshumedeste* (The convert woman), and *Der mamzer* (The bastard). Shneour's Hebrew translations (some of which were probably the work of a ghost translator) never found the success in Palestine/Israel as they had in Europe and North America, and so by the 1950s his fame as a Hebrew writer was almost entirely based on the strength of his poetry, while in Yiddish his prose had all but overshadowed his poems.

Readers of English looking for a taste of Shneour's later works can find a good selection in Moshe Spiegel's anthology, *Restless Spirit: Selected Writings of Zalman Shneour* (Thomas Yoseloff, 1963).

◆

I would like to thank Batia Baum, Judy Feldmann, Daniel Hahn, Bill Johnston, Eitan Kensky, Fleur Kuhn-Kennedy, Marc Lowenthal, Yitskhok Niborski, Larry Rosenwald, Katherine Silver, the 2016 Translation Fellows at the Yiddish Book Center, and the 2018 prose-workshop participants at the BCLT summer school for advice, feedback, and encouragement at various stages of the translation process.

Daniel Kennedy
*Rennes, August 2018*

## NOTES

1.  Zalman Reyzen, *Leksikon fun der yidisher literatur prese un filologye*, vol. 4 (Vilna: Farlag B. Kletskin, 1929), 807–820.

2.  Dan Miron. "Shneour, Zalman," in *YIVO Encyclopedia of Jews in Eastern Europe*, 2010, http://www.yivoencyclopedia.org/article.aspx/Shneour_Zalman.

3.  Shachar Pinsker, "Warsaw in Hebrew Literature 1880–1920: New Perspectives," *Studia Judaica* 35, no. 1 (2015): 111.

4.  Reyzen, *Leksikon*.

5.  Naomi Brenner, *Lingering Bilingualism: Modern Hebrew and Yiddish Literatures in Contact* (Syracuse University Press, 2016), 129.

6.  Most famously, *Margaritleklekh*.

7.  *Litvak* literally means "Lithuanian Jew" but refers to a group whose regional identity was considerably older and more stable than the borders of Eastern Europe, living in the area roughly equivalent to modern-day Lithuania, Latvia, Belarus, and parts of northeast Poland. The Litvaks differed from the Poylish (Polish) Jews and Galitsyaner (Galician/Ukrainian) Jews in dialect, cuisine, and temperament.

8.  Y. D. Berkowitz, *Undzere rishoynim* (Tel-Aviv, 1966), 138.

9.  Brenner, *Lingering Bilingualism*, 125.

10.  Nethanel Lilach, "David Vogel's Lost Hebrew Novel, *Viennese Romance*," *Prooftexts* 33, no. 3 (2013): 331.

11.  Alison Schachter, *Diasporic Modernisms* (Oxford University Press, 2012), 80.

# A DEATH

# CHAPTER 1

---

I've been hiding it for almost two weeks now, right here in my pocket, the instrument of my ultimate demise; the slaughtering blade of the Angel of Death: the revolver.

My revolver is smooth and as cold as death itself, and when I gaze into its deep, dark barrel I feel the Angel of Death, eternal and mute, staring back at me with one of its thousand eyes, glaring as only the empty eye sockets of a skull can glare. And I could almost swear that I see—suspended in the air—a set of clenched, dead teeth smiling at me.

Really, though, it's all quite pathetic; they took one type of metal and mixed it with another, molded it into a specific shape, attached a spring, then added a couple of screws to some oblong strips of lead. And the whole thing weighs only a pound—one measly pound! The device itself is quite small. It's simple, naïve and cold. But just try it, my dear brother; give the little contraption a squeeze, with one finger in just the right place, and it'll treat you to a bang, spewing out smoke and fire! You'll feel how much hatred that bang contains, hatred for you and everything alive. And this mute, little machine will *kill* people: large people, clever people, jolly people, and stupid people. It will kill happy people and sad people; people who have spent many, many years cultivating their bodies and minds; people who have seen a lot and suffered a lot, who have eaten and drunk a lot; those who have experienced much pain and much joy, and who go to sleep at night secure in the knowledge that they'll wake up again the next morning, as usual, and continue to live, eat, and tell lies, drinking in the best life has to offer while spitting out the worst. Go ahead, give this finely crafted pound of metal just one small squeeze and—poof! Anyone standing in the path of the round, black hole will collapse, knocked to the ground with paralyzed limbs, the strength fading from their muscles, and everything that they've ever seen and read and heard, collected and absorbed over decades with strain and toil, will become irrelevant, lost forever in that one split second.

Personally, I derive sweet pleasure from having such an ingenious little device, a machine that can command death itself, in my pocket. All I have to do is wish for it and my revolver will fire and murder. And should I not wish for it, it will sit there quietly in my back pocket, playing dumb, acting innocent. The little bastard!

I've got death itself in my pocket and I am its master, its commander: like clay in a potter's hand, so death is in mine.

I return to my lodgings in the evening, tired and broken after my hours of teaching, hours that stretch out like years. I search for something to invigorate me, but I find nothing. My books have long been coated in a layer of dust, and the tea stinks of oil. The bread is no longer fresh, and the butter is rancid. Then I lock the door of my room and slowly take out my weapon—my dear, sweet revolver. I lay it down on the table in front of me, and then I carry it over to the pillow. *That's a nice, soft bed for it; it feels more comfortable there.* I adore looking at it from every angle. I caress its smooth, polished back, while, on the wall behind me, my large, black shadow does the same thing. I think I hear death itself jumping around inside that hollow instrument like a wicked, mute little ghost trying to break free from its metal prison. It longs to escape, to shoot and kill, to split skulls, and bore holes through hearts and through the sides of people's heads. With vicious malice it watches me through the dark, narrow hole, and its glare—the glare of an empty eye in a dead skull—talks to me.

"Let me go," it says. "You should let me go free!"

Then my teeth clench involuntarily; I hiss through them a few broken, unwieldy words, the kind of words you'd speak in a fever, or during a wild, spontaneous celebration: I whisper to my gun, which lies glistening on the pillow:

"Listen, you little bastard, it won't kill you to wait another week, another two weeks, there'll be time enough for carnage."

And fearfully, lest death breaks ranks and starts firing to spite me, in case it loses control of itself from so much built-up malice and does me in before it's time, I hurry to lock it up in its thick leather holster; like those shirts you put on madmen, this is my revolver's straitjacket.

It is a strange thing to admit, but it makes me think of my dead father. That tall, thin Jew would turn pale and start trembling at the mere sight of a weapon; he'd be afraid to touch it, as if it were on fire. Whereas here I am—the son of that weak, nervous man—getting along so well with a loaded gun, keeping it always in my pocket, constantly feeling its pleasing weight against my thigh. It feels as if there's a second, secret heart beating inside it, beating in time with my own. How I love it! With what deep passion I feel its smooth shiny metal in my hand. I'm convinced that this is the same passion with which men caress the soft, smooth arms of their lovers—though that's something I myself have never experienced.

There are warm nights, full of heavy shadows and nightmares that choke me and keep me from sleeping; on those nights I remove the gun from its sheath and press its cool metal to my burning cheek. In the darkness, my dry lips twist into a strange, quiet smile.

Inspired by the movements of my lips, the shadows and nightmares that had been oppressing me duplicate my smile, breaking into a grin as strange and silent as my own. How many nights do I doze off to sleep like this until morning, my cheek pressed fast against the revolver. And when I awaken there it is on my pillow in the pale morning light—warm, smooth, silent. It smiles a shiny metallic smile at me.

But under its honest mask, I feel a dark, hidden life, a wild, hidden desire to shoot and kill ... Then I throw it a scornful glance, the scowl of an adult catching a child in a forbidden act. I pout, sternly sticking out my bottom lip, and wag my finger at it.

"Hey now, behave yourself, you little bastard. The Devil won't carry you off if you have to wait another week ... another two weeks.

◆

I believe I'm beginning to understand my unusual mental state of this past year. I've been feeling an urge to read both the local and the provincial *faits divers* in the newspapers, where I often find detailed descriptions of people who have done themselves harm. I lap those stories up quietly, with a secret thirst, locking myself away in my room, as with some perversion that demands privacy. Each of those morbid cases, printed so callously in tiny, uneven letters, fuels my fantasy for a long time. I imagine clearly—picturing with colors so vivid they hurt—the preparations involved in such deaths. Then, the act of killing itself: the bodies of poisoned suicides, flapping about, unable to scream through burning throats and lips; the outstretched legs of the hanged, their long, long necks; ropes swinging in the air after the door has been broken open and the noose has been cut ... then, wounded temples, foreheads with dark blue circular holes, brains through which a hot, metal bullet has passed ...

And as I read, I always try to conjure up a clear feeling about each of the different kinds of deaths that can transform a living person into a carcass.

Here they are:

(a) *Poison*: a cold fire in liquid form flows through your esophagus, twists your intestines into convulsions, dries up your stomach juices, and eats its way through the warm walls of your gut. There are needles in your stomach, multiplying with each passing minute until they overpower every drop of blood, every vein and artery, eventually reaching your brain. Each vein screams in fierce, mute pain; a million barbed needles penetrate, burn, and stab ...

(b) *Hanging*: Just one small kick and the stool falls out from under you—the strong, smooth noose, lubricated with soap, instantly grabs your fragile neck like a pair of iron pliers. Your neck muscles soon lose their power and flexibility—they cannot save your outstretched neck, they cannot hold on. Your body becomes seventy-seven times heavier, pulling you down without mercy ... the daylight turns cloudy-white as though mixed with milk, then green, then black; the veins in your temples pound as if with pointed hammers; with a terrible anguish your lungs flounder like fish pulled living out of the water; your brain is on the verge of bursting under the strong current of blood which has no means of escape; the tips of your feet twitch ever so slightly, barely noticeable, like a steel spring, winding down—one more moment, and ...

(c) *Drowning*: a sudden fall from an arched bridge so high it makes your head spin; trees, buildings, people, and carriages flip and become blurred as you lose consciousness—the frigid wetness of the water . . . *brrr* . . . in less than a second your lungs are filled up like sacks, right up to your throat. Your body grows heavy, and sinks; your nostrils and mouth instinctively continue to breathe, dragging in more and more water, instead of fresh, sweet air . . . your eyes swell up, and see only a green, merciless emptiness and void.

There is a muffled roar in your submerged ears. Your lungs shudder, trying to expel the water they've swallowed, which presses like cold lead against their delicate, weak walls—they cannot. A wild scream tries to escape, but—instead of air—liquid rushes in, and the scream is stifled amid horrifying torture.

(d) *Shooting*: The cool, round, metal object presses itself against your warm temple. A signal runs down your spine; your finger touches the right spot—your brain is working normally, fueling the nerves and feelings when suddenly—bang!

Your skull explodes with a wet slap, like an elastic bone; the sharp, oblong "guest" darts through your brain, rending and tearing everything with incomparable agony. The brain, father of all muscles, sensations, veins, and nerves, feels in one short second the hellish pain that all the muscles and nerves together would have felt if they'd been slowly sawed to the point of snapping—all that diabolical suffering in one, all-encompassing spasm . . . and then it's over.

That's how I imagined and reimagined every grisly case. I read about all manner of suicides which the heroes of the daily newspapers had chosen for themselves. I thought about them day and night, embellishing the accounts with details from my own imagination. The constant stream of morbid ideas was making a fatalist of me. Everything around me stoked my macabre fixations: If I happened to walk past a high wall, I would think to myself, *that wall could start to wobble at this very moment and collapse, flattening me like a beefsteak.* Or I'd be walking across the iron bridge that spans high over the breadth of the river. *That water flowing past, so slow and seemingly docile, could drown me! This shiny knife, sharpened to slice bread, could just as well be used to kill, and could quite easily stab me, right here and now; it only needs to know under which rib my heart lies.*

Once I stood and craned my neck to look at the inscription on a high monument. Towering proudly over me was the figure in question, a large, fat-bellied general, cast entirely in bronze. Next to him, I looked so small and alone. It occurred to me that the monument could, at any moment, fall and crush me under its hundred-pound weight. A concealed, animalistic instinct of self-preservation, triggered by the mere possibility that it could fall and kill me, impelled me to jump aside out from under the shadow of the statue. But I soon felt that my fear was foolish, if not insane. I stepped forward, out of spite, back into the shadow of the statue, standing even closer to it than before. A wide, foolish smile spread over my lips as I addressed the pot-bellied bronze general.

"Well, come on then . . . go ahead and fall. Crush me. I'd like to see you try."

On another occasion, one foggy morning, I heard the news that an old childhood friend of mine, twenty-two years old, had poisoned himself. He had drunk down a bottle of carbolic acid, which he'd bought himself at the pharmacy. I could not sit still the whole day and wandered around in a kind of sweet distress. My imagination dwelled on the idea of a death like that, enlarging it as though under a microscope to many times its actual size.

Indeed, that very evening, as I was wandering pensively through the streets, I suddenly gave my pockets a tap to see if I had a few coins. Finding that I did, I went, not knowing how I got there, to a pharmacy and said, short of breath, "Ten kopecks worth of phenol."

And as I came out into the street clutching the bottle, wrapped in blotting paper, between my cold fingers, I suddenly looked at it, surprised, and asked myself: "What the Devil do I need this for anyway?"

After some thought, I hurled the bottle against the pavement where it shattered into tiny pieces. A light plume of smoke and several pink bubbles rose from the spot where it had landed. I stared at the smoke from the carbolic acid, and smiled as it dispersed in the air.

And then there was another incident, more pathetic still. One time I was out walking, ruminating for the tenth time on a story I'd read concerning a young man who had hanged himself in his room, on a hook attached to a beam. I suddenly remembered that there was also a hook hanging from the ceiling of my own room that could be used to hang oneself.

I had a moment of doubt; *perhaps I was wrong? Maybe there was no such hook in my room?* I set off immediately homeward. I arrived and, yes, there it was: a solid, iron hook, curved inward with a tip like an eagle's beak, like the crooked fang of a Devil, right there in the center of the ceiling. It whispered to me, *You could hang yourself on me, yes indeed you could.*

"Well I'll be damned," I said to myself. "How could I not have noticed it until now? A strong, pointy, iron hook, I'll be damned!"

It stood out against the whitewashed ceiling, black, hungry, and ready—beckoning. My lips broke into a thin smile, as I addressed the hook in a whisper, "Is that so? Really? You mean it? Someone could hang themselves on you? Very interesting. Let's see then."

I immediately sought out the rope I use to tie up my things whenever I move to new lodgings, and, with detached curiosity, I made myself a strong noose. I positioned a stool in the middle of the room and was on the verge of attaching the other end of the rope to the iron hook.

*I will soon hang myself*, I thought calmly, my head wrapped in a passionate fog. *I swear it, I will hang myself.*

Suddenly there was a knock at the door. My unnatural serenity vanished in an instant and I was bathed in a cold sweat. I was struck by the gravity of what I was about to do, and the danger that it entailed. In the blink of an eye, I hid the rope and hastily returned the stool to its usual spot.

"Who is it?"

"It's me."

It was Merl Rivkin, a good-natured girl of my acquaintance. She had come to retrieve a book she'd lent me. When I opened the door, she stared at me with eyes like a pair of question marks. Her face was pale; apparently the sight of my sweaty countenance bore witness to the secret I had been trying to hide. Her gentle woman's heart sensed the strange deed I had been about to carry out, a deed that still hovered in the stagnant air of my room, ashamed and uncomfortable, like an inept burglar caught in the act.

Once my acquaintance had left, I took a knife and cut the rope into tiny pieces. Cutting that rope gave me a strange feeling of satisfaction: the feeling of a bitter man taking vengeance on his own hatred, catching and destroying his would-be predator.

Nevertheless, I was agitated for days. I would stare up at the bent hook in the ceiling until I was exhausted. At night, once I had put out the lamp, I could no longer see it. But I could sense it there in the dark. It seemed to breathe, expanding and contracting, and it kept me awake. Eventually I rented myself a new room where there was no hook hanging from the ceiling, and I could relax.

But not for long.

I made a new acquaintance: a muscular young man, with a solid, pockmarked face. He worked as a bookkeeper in an ironworks factory. One evening, as I was sitting at his place drinking tea, he put his hand into his wide pocket and produced a beautiful, polished revolver. He pointed its dark barrel directly at me, laughed and said: "Bam! Now I'll kill you."

I did not tremble as he had expected. I merely sat there, frozen, and stared ardently at the beautiful weapon. But afterward, as I held it in my hands to look at it, and my fingers touched its cold, smooth nickel surface, a shudder passed through my whole body. At that very second, the riddle that had long been weighing on my mind became clear. I suddenly knew with my whole being that I must possess that shining object—*I must use any pretext to make it mine.*

Unable to contain myself, I set about trying to convince my acquaintance, speaking feverishly.

"Listen, my friend, sell me your revolver, you'll be doing me an enormous favor. I'll pay you in cash, please. I simply must have it, you understand?"

He looked at me skeptically, "What do you need it for, exactly?"

I felt that I'd over-egged it, and was somewhat bewildered. I didn't yet know what I wanted it for. Nevertheless I composed myself, and I could hear my own voice speaking in a disinterested tone, but the words seemed to come out all wrong.

"Things are happening, all around, you know what I mean? Pogroms, people being attacked, murdered ... everyone needs to protect themselves, don't they?"

My acquaintance's expression returned to normal. Through one half of his mouth, he muttered a price for the shiny object. Then he grew agitated, practically swearing that he was joking, that he himself had paid a lot more for it, but that either way, he did not want to hang on to it any more, and for a friend, well, long story short: let's say fifteen rubles!

I knew that he was lying. But I did not try to haggle. In fact, I was grateful. My lips all but shivered with gratitude. I did not have any money on me, so I left, determined to get some. My heart beat wildly as I contemplated the beautiful weapon sitting in a stranger's pocket. I asked my acquaintance not to sell it to anyone else in the meantime. God forbid. It was *mine*.

The next day I managed to get an advance for one of the lessons I teach. I still owed money for food and rent, but I did not care. I set off as early as possible to see the young man who had *my* revolver.

When I arrived with the money I found his door locked. Two long hours I waited for him on the street next to the gate. A wintry drizzle started to fall. The pavement was wet. Iron roof-tiles began glinting with dampness, and I waited, shivering. My throat was dry and bitter. Finally I saw the man approach. I restrained myself from rushing to meet him.

"Ah, you've come about the thing? Already? What's the hurry?"

He set about questioning me in a leisurely fashion, with the smile of one who can sense another man's weakness and insecurity.

I stared back at him with a mute prayer in my eyes, hoping that all was not ruined. What could I say? Admittedly, I myself was at a loss to explain my eagerness to have the gun, or why it had so aroused me. I understood that during such a transaction, one should remain calm. But I could not.

After he took the money, he did not hand over the weapon immediately. He gave me the pleasure of showing me how to use it, how to load the bullets, and how to take it apart, piece by piece, with each hidden screw.

My heart raced as he handled the revolver, as if I were witnessing an operation being performed on my own child before my eyes.

I was afraid, *what if, God forbid, he damages something, or drops a screw?* But nothing happened. Oh, he was quite a fellow all right, he knew how to handle a gun.

Finally he passed it to me, with warning after warning: "Treat it with care, don't let anyone know you have it; that's all I need is the police to come knocking on my door . . ." and so on.

With an impatience that could have aroused suspicion, I set off at once, alone, to a spot just outside the city. The whole way I fingered and caressed my lovely new revolver until it became warm. It seemed as if I had roused an unseen life inside its cold, dead metal.

Drops of rain still hung on the grass, wetting my shoes. The day was coming to an end, wrapped in bloody clouds of various shapes and in every shade of red. The field was large, green, and empty.

Then, eagerly, I slowly slid my revolver out of its sheath and began to commune with it.

I regarded it with deep grateful passion, unable to believe my own eyes: *looks as though it's mine! mine . . .*

I got ready to fire it into the air, as a test. The whole field seemed to be waiting in breathless expectation. Distant trees leaned forward, curious to see: *what will happen? what will happen?*

I fired.

On the face of it, not much happened A small thunderclap tore out along with a puff of bluish smoke, which gradually dispersed in the damp, brisk evening air. And yet . . . the Devil take it! No thunderclap had ever shaken me as much as that shot. I heard several muffled echoes coming at me from all sides, the whole field seemed to shake, and stare at me in fear. I imagined I heard in that bang a dark, terrible laughter, a distant echo from the next world.

Wet blades of grass licked my shoes and a giant, cold, red sun went down behind the blood-red mist, seemingly outraged that the sudden gunfire had disturbed its final moments of glorious, stately peace.

# CHAPTER 2

THE 25TH OF ELEL

*That* idea! How exactly had it managed to lodge itself in my heart? When did it come to me? Was it born at the same time I was? Or had it slowly grown without my feeling it? I cannot recall.

What I do remember is that I was something of a strange child: quiet and sullen, tending to stay indoors by myself. I was pale, and prone to colds. I would lie with my swollen throat wrapped in a woolen sock filled with warm salt, and let my mind wander for hours. My sickly thoughts, young, lonely, and without form, drifted like a murky fog, without purpose, like the autumn clouds that drench the earth, day and night, without nourishing it. The clouds themselves don't know why they make their way across the sky, why they drip cold water down onto the earth, and the earth does not know why it needs the water. And yet it accepts the rain, drinking it lazily, growing too soft and too damp, until it can do nothing but splatter with mud. Similarly, I did not know why I was compelled to think. What good was the endless drip-drop of ideas? But think I did.

The air in our silent, desolate house was always filled with cold shadows, the walls adorned with banal, faded pictures. The house was crammed full of old, bulky furniture, tasteless and chaotic, entirely lacking in coziness or warmth. "Bargains" the lot of it, the likes of which you find occasionally in special sales, sold off by homeowners who were leaving for America. It all stood there, aging, growing sepulchral in the shadows, leaving no space to breathe, all of which fed into my temperament. The house offered up its treasures for my sole benefit: its atmosphere, its odious walls, its tastelessness, tedium, and silence—all so I could think my gloomy thoughts, safe and undisturbed. Our derelict house, lonely and silent, was a part of my thoughts and my thoughts were a part of the house; each seemingly engendering and nourishing the other.

When my health improved somewhat, my father—a widower—and our elderly maid Brayne would talk to me, encouraging me to play and be more like other children. I'd return, lazy and dissatisfied, to my playthings, which I never really took care of and never really mistreated. And deep in my heart I yearned for the times when I was sick, for the warm woolen sock around my neck, for my blankets and for the strange musings that come from too much bed rest.

I did not like children of my own age, nor did I hate them. I regarded them with an unhealthy indifference bordering on disgust. Our maid, moved by my loneliness, would sometimes invite the neighbors' children to the house to play with me. But I refused to go near them. I'd just sit there, staring sadly.

"Go on, play!" Brayne would encourage me, before resuming her work in the kitchen.

The children would look at me with curiosity at first, timidly gnawing on their fingers, as though I were an adult. Then they'd slowly approach—a step forward followed by a glance, another step, another glance—and cautiously begin to play with the toys that lay near me on the floor. I would not move an inch. They'd propose a game with my wooden horse or my little wagon and I would blurt out, half in shame, half in anger: "Leave me alone!" before falling silent once more.

The children would soon get bored, and frown at me with eyes full of childish scorn, pouting, as if I'd offended them somehow; then suddenly, for no reason, they'd burst into tears, crying aloud: "We want to go home . . . home . . . home."

I have no memory of my mother because she died giving birth to me. She left no pictures of herself behind.

My father—a tall, not especially clever man with a soft ruddy beard—was affectionate in his way. But he was always occupied with his work as a grain-dealer. The burden of the business lay entirely on his shoulders; he had no employees. He did not go in for ledgers, books, notes, logs, or accounts. In place of double-entry bookkeeping he had only his tired brain, a mass of mobile wrinkles on his sunburned brow, and many, many scraps of paper covered in lists and pencil marks. The pockets of his vest, trousers, and coat were always stuffed with such papers in all imaginable formats, which came spilling out whenever he removed his handkerchief.

The town beyond the walls of our house, a provincial town in Lithuania, would swallow him up for the whole day. He would eat lunch in a hurry, slurping and gobbling, unable to sit still, before heading back out. He'd come home late at night when the shutters had long been lowered. I slept in my mother's old bed, which had remained next to my father's since her death. As soon as my father came in, he would approach my bed, his face pale, and ask in a soft, hoarse voice:

"Shloymke, are you asleep?"

As a sickly child all alone at home I'd long grown used to sleeping during the day, and so afterward I would not be able to fall asleep until late at night.

"No."

I never succeeded in speaking much with my father; he was a difficult man to approach. And I found it hard to utter the word "father"; I avoided it whenever I could.

"No?" he'd ask, with nothing particular in mind, his tall body looming over me, and pull the blanket up as far as my nose.

"Go to sleep!" he'd say, "sleep through the night."

And for the next half hour I'd listen to him, pulling off his long boots in the darkness of the bedroom, throwing them under the bed as carefully as he could, and begin muttering distractedly to himself with half words:

"Hmm . . . It's time I reckon . . . certainly time . . . he's been sick so long . . . every indication . . . if you can't, you can't . . . promissory notes . . . and Epshteyn's bills—unpaid? Not there yet? . . . can you fathom it? . . . If you say nothing, eh? Again . . . nothing to be done . . . aha . . . yes . . . it's possible . . . quite possible . . ."

I loved to listen to these fragmentary utterances and picture him furrowing his brow in the darkness as he spoke.

Until finally, after a good while chattering to himself, he'd let out a sigh and lie down on his big mattress; his tired brain would suddenly sense someone listening. He would lift his head and ask as he usually did:

"Shloymke, are you asleep?"

"No."

"Go to sleep!"

Often, some time after these brief exchanges, I'd be overcome by a childish fear. *Where am I anyway?*

I'd begin pleading quietly, still not daring to say the word "father": "Light the lamp! Light the lamp!"

Instead of a reply, I'd hear my father's tired, ragged snoring. Then I'd hide my head under the blanket, block my ears, and wouldn't say another word.

◆

One evening, my father returned home earlier than usual. His face seemed different; the worried wrinkles on his brow had straightened. There was a small, hidden joy in his usually dispirited eyes. He paced back and forth through the house, his legs rubbing together as he walked, clasping his frozen hands together—though it was a cold, white winter outside, he seemed to do so out of distraction rather than on account of the chill.

I sat on my little chair, my cold throat wrapped in its habitual woolen sock. For several minutes all was quiet.

My heart told me that at any moment my father would speak. And suddenly, he did in fact walk up to me and ask me a question.

"Shloymele, do you remember what your mother's name was?

I was taken aback and looked up at him with childish curiosity.

He seemed not to have anticipated such a look. He was disconcerted, and awkwardly raised his voice:

"Don't you remember your mother's name? Eh? No?"

His voice frightened me, and I burst into tears.

But he just bent down, and repeated confusedly:

"Come on now, Nekhome was her name, there's no need to cry . . . Nekhome, Nekhome . . . you silly thing. It was Nekhome! . . ."

The name Nekhome stirred memories of large, kindly, blue eyes and a smooth gracious brow under a black wig with a white parting down the middle. Where had I seen that face? How did I know about it? Was it Nekhome, my mother? Who had described her to me? My father? The maid?

My childhood was not rich in impressions, in words or games, in images or sounds, so I'd developed a habit of repeating words and half words that appealed to me. After the conversation with my father, as I played with my little wooden soldier, I caressed its head, playfully flicking its painted nose, and attempted to mimic my father's voice:

"Come on now, Nekhome, you silly thing, Nekhome … Nekhome I'm telling you. What are you crying about now?"

Late that same night, my father took me into his bed beside him—again: this was unusual—and spoke:

"Would you like to have a mother here? A new mother … like Nekhome … she will also be kind … she'll buy you sweets … Would you like that, son?"

I said nothing.

"She'll cook nice things. Our maid Brayne can't cook the likes … she can't. Ah, she'll make good pudding, kugel with raisins … You like kugel with raisins?

"Kugel with raisins … ," I repeated in a dull voice, pulling away from my father. And my little heart began telling prophecies in the dark.

"In summer she'll take you for walks in the public gardens … You know, the park … you'd like that, eh? She'll be a good mother, yeah?

"Yeah," I echoed weakly. Then my father picked me up carefully in his arms, like a baby, carried me back to my bed, tucked me in, and said in his usual manner: "Go to sleep."

But I lay there in the darkness for a long time, my eyes open, whispering to myself:

"Kugel with raisins … kugel with raisins … Nekhome … walks in the gardens … Nekhome … Nekhome …"

◆

A big-nosed Jewess, with large, drooping breasts, a fat, withered face with crude features, bloodshot eyes, and no eyebrows arrived and took up residence in our big empty house. She brought with her a wagon-load of cushions, quilts, and pillows, and by the time all the bedding had been taken in and added to our own ample supply the air in every room was thick with fine particles of down and feathers.

A porter carried the things into our house while the portly Jewess, my new stepmother, raced around, exhausted and sweaty, shouting incessantly in a hoarse, ringing voice: "There are more cushions . . . that's not the last of them . . . carry them in . . ." looking for all the world like a chicken about to be sacrificed for Yom Kippur.

I was sick, as usual, and that night I had strange dreams. I dreamt that our whole house was being entirely stuffed full of cushions and quilts until I began to drown under a sea of dust and feathers, unable to scream. From one minute to the next the cavity of our house was filled with bedding. Soon it reached the windows, then it covered our glass cabinets, before long it would reach the ceiling. And my stepmother, fat and sweaty, dancing over the cushions commanded in a shrill voice: "More cushions . . . that's not the last of them . . . keep carrying them in . . ."

They removed my bed from the room I used to share with my father, and set me up in the dining room on the sofa. From that day forward my father's relationship with me changed. When he came home late at night and walked past my bed, he would address me in the dark:

"Shloymke, are you asleep?"

"No."

But he would no longer come over to tuck me in as he used to; he would merely tell me to go to sleep, more out of habit than out of love, and head straight to the bedroom.

In my childish heart I knew that she, she alone, whom I was now expected to call "aunt" or better still, "mother," was responsible for the change in my father's comportment.

In the cool darkness of our large quarters I often heard my father speaking to *her* as he removed his boots and threw them under the bed. In those moments I was so jealous of that ample woman; I yearned for my mother's bed where I'd slept until now; for the way my father would gasp just before he drifted off to sleep; his gentle, gravelly voice, which would sometimes address me. Silently I grew to hate, truly to despise the woman who'd stolen it all away from me. She was so restrained, so apathetic; she never spoke to me, never exchanged a word.

But I had no opportunity to openly display my hatred toward this strange interloper; her behaviour toward me was neither cold nor warm. That amorphous bag, who would break into a sweat at even the slightest effort, barely noticed that I existed at all, seemingly oblivious to the pale child wandering around the house with a woolen sock tied around his neck. On those occasions when I met her watery gaze, it was lethargic and indifferent: the sort of gaze an earnest person usually reserves for household pets.

She would often forget to look at me at all, only remembering my existence when it was time to eat or sleep:

"Shloymke, food! Shloymke, bedtime!..."

That's how one treats a cat too, you throw it a bone and call it over: here puss, puss, puss.

By that time, I was learning in *kheyder* and when one day the teacher dropped by to collect the tuition fees my father chatted with him while *she* lounged on the sofa, yawning with a wide, withered mouth, not saying a single word.

If I happened to ask her something, she would slowly raise her red eyes, which expressed nothing at all, and respond with a yawn:

"Wh-ah-ah at? . . ."

Often whole days went by without either of us saying a word to each other. So it continued, for days, months, years, and our relationship, without an ounce of love or a drop of animosity, washed over me with coldness and the stench of the grave. My heart felt battered, darkened, neglected; it hid away somewhere in a corner of my breast, growing ever less capable of producing, or receiving, any genuine emotion.

The animosity I harbored toward her stagnated; starved of sustenance by her behavior, it became as though covered in rust. Eventually, I began to regard her with the same lack of feeling as she did me.

I'd return in the evening after a day at *kheyder* and sit in my old chair warming my hands by the stove. On one such evening I recall gazing into the burning wood and seeing fiery little men winking at me from inside, sticking out their tiny, hellish red and blue tongues. The fire cast fantastical shadows on the walls and on the old furniture, which danced along with the flames . . . The stale smell of tedium hung in the air, the odor of loneliness, of the humdrum, of aimlessness accompanied by another smell: the smell of my stepmother herself, her hazy negligence. My father had not yet returned from town. My stepmother was dozing right in the middle of the sofa, where her weight had broken several springs; her nose whistled. I was alone, all alone in the desolate, silent house, with nothing but my childish soul and dreary imagination. What thoughts passed through my mind! Nature abhors a vacuum, and so thoughts flowed into my mind, just as wild thorny weeds will grow in a field when one neglects to sow it.

I never had anyone with whom I could share my inner thoughts. In my imagination everything I'd ever seen, heard, learned, or understood took on exaggerated forms, ugly and dreadful. Everything around me felt immobile, paralyzed. The walls, the furniture, the very air in the rooms: it all pressed against me, everything conspiring to freeze my heart, and petrify my feelings. I longed with every limb, with my whole being for my stepmother to start nagging me, torturing me, scolding me, heaping every possible curse upon my head (as I've heard stepmothers are supposed to do according to the stories of my classmates) so that I could be permitted to hate her, to answer her back, to make her life miserable . . . I ached for her to beat me, to dole out punches, pull my hair, so that I could throw my old galoshes in her face. I could pour pitch into her new hat. I could tear up her quilts, as large and thick as she was, bigger even . . . our whole house would be filled with feathers. Afterward I would run off to the prayer house, and spend the night there on a bench.

Such vengeful thoughts brought me an especially sweet pain. Only the hungry—those who have not eaten for several days, fantasizing about a piece of fried goose, whose odor reaches them from afar—are familiar with such sweet suffering.

◆

I was about ten years old. We were learning Mishnah in *kheyder* one warm Shabbes afternoon when we came to the phrase: "*Marbe boser marbe rime*,"—"One who increases his flesh, increases worms." The teacher was drinking tea. His shirt was unbuttoned, revealing a hairy chest. He was sweating, his face wrinkled with pleasure as he taught us the interpretation of the text, explaining that each worm that feeds on a corpse causes pain like a needle in living flesh. I brought my boyish hands under the table, pinched my skinny little knees, and immediately a thought flashed into my mind: *I will die, it's certain that I will die, but the worms will not sting me much. They won't get much out of me: I'm too skinny . . . but my stepmother? Oho! She's so big and fat . . . she'll be a feast for many worms. It's going to sting her all right, so many, many needles . . .*

The thought transported me into such a frenzy that, as soon as the lesson was over, I hurried to confide in my friend Yosl.

"You know, the worms will only eat me a little, only a little, but my 'Aunt'—Oho!"

Yosl, a crafty, cross-eyed lad, felt it necessary to embellish the image by adding: "Just like the carcass we saw that time in the hollow under the tree, remember?"

"Yes . . . but the worms won't eat me."

"Oh, but you might get fat yet; my father told me that can happen—you'll be fat with a long beard."

My mood darkened. I frowned at Yosl for stealing my joy. Yet I answered him with an inner confidence: "No, no, I'll never get fat, never. You'll see, never."

My voice took on the clarity and authority of an adult's. Yosl started; he looked at me in silent wonder. In that moment, my face must have expressed something that Yosl had never seen on the faces of boys his own age. I returned home, my head spinning with confused thoughts. I sat down in my habitual corner without asking for food and remained there, alone with my sad young thoughts.

The sun was beginning to set. Golden flecks of sunlight wandered across the walls, clambering over the furniture. The house was empty. My father had gone to afternoon prayers, leaving behind a still warm glass of tea on the table. The maid had gone out for some fresh air. Only my stepmother was left, drowsing on the sofa, her face so sweaty it was painful to behold. She did not glance at me as I entered, merely asked in a dazed stupor: "Who's there?" before drifting back to sleep.

In addition to the endless boredom and solitude in the house, there now hung that sad, oppressive emptiness that creeps into the soul when one passes from the holy to the profane, from a holiday atmosphere to the everyday, that emptiness that one feels after a lengthy celebration, such as on the trip home after a wedding.

I always felt this melancholy as Shabbes was coming to an end. And in our home, full as it was of sloth and isolation, the melancholy flowed stronger, like a contagious disease, like bacteria that are fruitful and multiply in the filth on which they gladly feast.

The sadness merged with the creeping shadows, becoming one gray mass, steadily besieging my young heart, which cowered in a dark corner.

Yet suddenly the stillness in our house was shattered. The wretched, drawn-out clang of a church-bell rang out, splitting the cool silence in two. The melancholy burst into many smaller fragments, which twirled around me, crawling on my hair, dancing around my head:

*Bim—bam, bim—bam . . .*

The growling clang seemed bent on startling us, warning us: "All is not well, all is not well . . . watch out! watch out!"

From the other direction, the dirgeful, protracted melody of the psalms from the nearby prayer house could still be heard:

*"Ashrey tmimey derekh hohoylkhim betoyres Adoynoy"*

The incantation of the psalms and the ringing of the church-bells became unwittingly entangled. In harmonious yearning the sound poured into the darkening room, stealing its way into my heart, and all at once I felt the full burden of my profound solitude. Moved almost to the point of tears, I longed more than anything for a soft, warm lap to lay my head on, for a warm mother's hand to caress my hair.

I had witnessed such a scene in Yosl's house: his mother was caressing his head in that gloomy twilight that coincides with the end of Shabbes, singing with a soft, weak voice before lighting a match: "*Got fun Avrom, fun Yitskhokn un fun Yankevn . . .*"

Oh, how I would love my stepmother if she held my head in her lap like that . . . If Nekhome were still alive, the real Nekhome, that's what she would do . . . but I'd also be contented with my step-mother's lap.

There she lay, my stepmother, on the sofa: fat, drenched in sweat, her limbs hanging limp and motionless.

I could not hold myself back and approached her, not know-ing what I was going to say.

"Mother . . . ? Aunt . . . ?"

I pictured Nekhome, two blue eyes under a matt wig with a part down the middle . . .

My *aunt* did not budge, did not so much as glance in my direction, only asked: "Are you hungry? Is that it?"

"No, no, never mind."

I took a step backward with a heavy heart, unsure of what to do next. Then I approached again, right up close; my face was aflame, my lips trembled.

"I know it's a lie . . ." I said. "A big lie . . . my father tricked me . . . you're nothing like a mother!"

"Hmm?"

"You're nothing like . . . like Nekhome!"

Her hairless brows rose, and her cold, beady eyes peered out with a watery shine.

"So what if I'm not?"

A wave of insolence and rage caught in my throat, bursting out in an unnatural, childish voice:

"You're an abomination! An abomination! You'll be eaten by worms . . . Abomination! . . ."

"Hush now, what is it? Are you hungry? Just a minute . . ."

And she clambered to her feet with a deep sigh, heading toward the kitchen to prepare me something to eat. She had not understood a thing. I felt ashamed, and for several days I could not bring myself to look her in the eye. Whenever she addressed me my cheeks turned red.

That was to be my first and last protest against the cold monotony and emptiness, my sole rebellion against the gray life in our home; a life that contained neither love, nor hate, nor purpose. My protest, as futile as it had been spontaneous, came to naught. Once again I was oppressed by the silence and tedium in the house which was only interrupted by the periodic clatter of knives and forks. Our tepid relationship continued to darken, settling on me, slow, constant, and thick, like a layer of dust.

My hatred grew stale, and I once again became as indifferent to my stepmother as she was to me.

◆

Then, one day, the rains came, bringing to a close several months of illness and terrible pain for my father.

He lay on the floor, surrounded by a group of women—no strangers to the work of weeping—moaning with jutting lips and hanging noses. Their lamentations were deafening and they blew into their handkerchiefs with hyperbolic vigor. I stood there, pale and cold, but I did not cry. The sound of the wailing pained my ears, but it did not surprise me; it was as though I'd been born and raised in such an environment. I was numb to the keening, and lost in my own thoughts. The long, cold body seemed so alien, new, and interesting to me: the sunken cheeks, the reddish-gray hair, and the wrinkles. I stared with intense, private fascination at the candles, which were burning near the dead man's head. By their flickering, yellow shine his blue lips appeared to move and speak ... I was disappointed when they wrapped the dead man's head in a black shroud ... it was all so strangely captivating! ... *Why are the women shrieking like that? It would be better if they were quiet; if it were still ... Candles burning straight, slender, and white; yellow flames, with bluish tongues in the center, dead blue lips trembling in their shine ... Why have they covered all the mirrors? What about all the cold, abandoned pots in the kitchen? It's all so excessive, so needless ...*

An old woman approached me and whispered in my ear:

"Cry, you silly thing! ... It's your father after all ... your father is dead."

But I did not cry, I only blushed violently and hid myself away in a corner until the shame subsided. I turned around again and observed the wailing, the mourners, my father's bearded face with the drooping brow, which I could feel under the black sheet, and I could not understand why I did not weep.

That night after the burial, as I lay down to sleep, my imagination could not shake the smell of death, the smell of medicines, carbolic acid, ice-packs which had been piling up in every room for months on end. Then suddenly a lucid thought took form in my weary brain: *I too will die, but not with a beard and moustache like my father had . . . I won't have furniture or a house . . . no women will cry for me; they will not blow their hanging noses in their handkerchiefs . . . Of course I will die, I'll die.*

Even now I'm certain that was the precise moment when my childish thoughts, which had hitherto wandered in my mind like a sparse, inchoate mist, began to acquire their first characteristic traits.

# CHAPTER 3

Now, as I record the events of my life and see those cold, silent details, drab as autumn shadows, written down in black and white, as I grapple with my memories, it strikes me that already the seed of that idea had been planted in my childhood. The atmosphere in our house, my relationship with my stepmother, my father's business always standing between us like an iron wall: all these things contributed to the growth of that cold *thing* that entered me, sinking into the depths of my soul, impossible now to dislodge.

Slowly the seed split and sprouted, growing until its roots ran deep, ripening until the time came to eat its sweet poisonous fruit, to bring it out and put it to use . . . why else would I have bought the revolver?

No, it didn't come to me suddenly. No great revolution in my inner world, as is often the case with suicides, gave rise to it. I had nowhere to fall from because I had never reached a high enough point. Minor occurrences and events, tedious little pains, a long chain of dark days—half awake, half asleep—an inner pride and constant outer shame, discomfort, ridicule; strong desires and weak hands . . . fragments of unrealized hope: all of it had slowly gutted and destroyed my natural desire to survive, turning me into a hollowed vessel, unfit to contain life.

Like a tree growing without sunlight, like thorns sprouting without rain, the idea flourished in my desolate heart. Back in my father's house, it took shape year by year, though I did not perceive it. Later, far from my father's house, it continued to grow, out in the world, in hunger and solitude, and yet I did not see its unmistakable form. But now it has grown ripe and stands before me in all its stubborn coldness, in all its stony, firmly minted details saying: "Abandon life."

And, alongside the idea, the will to do the thing itself also matured: to transform the insubstantial impulse into a deed . . . At this very moment, for example, I'm lying on the sofa, yawning, and nothing in the world interests me. But, one morning, bright or dark, I might very well rise, take out the revolver, glance one last time at those sickeningly overfamiliar walls, always peering in through the window, and fire into my breast, or my temple—my hand will not tremble, my heart will not race. Yes, I can feel it! And I'm happy I have the key to it. The key to death is in my hand.

Those austere strangers who run around in the streets, who have not yet lived through this day and are already worrying about tomorrow, if they only knew what was going on inside me, the thoughts I harbor, and the shiny object I have in my pocket. Some of them would smile at me with dull optimism, others would pity me, but all would think: "A madman!" So be it, I consider their lives to be a form of madness. The main thing is the purpose behind it all: they have a reason to live and I have a reason to die. It turns out that I'm quite a special little truth unto myself and they are a larger more general truth unto themselves. There are many ideals and truths in this world, which are very far from one another. Each ideal hates the other; each faith cannot stand its neighbor, and yet each one remains strong and secure, because each contains its own truth.

It's almost pleasant to move through the streets with this feeling of death deep in my heart. My body, my natural movements, my entire form—it's all no more than a thick, hard shell wrapped around this hidden idea. Everything rushes around me, moving, searching, rushing, growling, whistling, and ringing, while here I am, a lump of death right at the center that life just can't seem to digest. I am frozen and calm. Only the cliff, standing in the middle of the raging sea, knows such calm. Waves rush, crashing against one another, driven half wild with so much power and energy, squabbling with each other, while the cliff stands there, its brow furrowed, and asks: "What does one need it all for? One could just stand still and be as stone."

"Why don't you run? Why don't you roar as hungrily as we do?" the waves ask it.

"I am stone," answers the cliff, "I have my own truth."

In two weeks, maybe in one, it'll all be too much for me; I'll be sick of standing here like this, watching others live, watching them rush and take and give—and then . . .

But there is still one score I have left to settle with life; I don't know if it's a big one or a small one. I only know that I have often yearned for it.

I don't want to leave this world without resolving it. I don't want—in my last moment before dying—to think that it's a mistake to throw away this "life" as they call it, while one part of it, a hidden part, full of secrets that I've never laid eyes upon, remains behind a dark curtain. I must taste it before death so that I may die without a shred of longing for this life I have so thoroughly discredited. I have known—in my scant years—hunger and fullness, hope and despair, good moods and bad, deep-rooted desire and unending, futile sadness, but there's one thing I have never known: a woman.

Today I am twenty years old, and I have not yet known a woman, a female, to put it bluntly. What will be will be. I will know one before I die!

Even as acquaintances I have known very few women in my life, but I have heard and read a lot about them. The printed version of woman, I know quite well, on paper at least . . .

And it has often pained me that I'm not even the merest shadow of one of the heroes in those novels, full of brooding passion and wonderful stories. It's often pained me that I can't sneak in through windows at night to meet countesses, notorious beauties, while their husbands are away from the palace. And it galls me to think that the only way for me to know a woman is by going *there* . . . to *that place* where I'll be obliged to buy a woman with pennies. But I'm not deluded; it's clear to me, that in such a house of ill fame I won't get anywhere near a real woman, as fiery and flexible as a snake, whimsical and tender, the woman of whom I've read so much, heard so much and dreamed so much . . .

But now, is it not all the same to me? I need only take care of my own needs, my natural, hidden instincts. Sex is only a little something extra on the side; death is the main coarse, which will come after the woman . . . I will carry it out with disgust, but I will carry it out. For pennies? Pennies it is, then. For pennies I used to buy bread and tea. For pennies I bought second-hand books with dog-eared pages. For pennies. When my sadness drove me to it I also bought joy for pennies: second-rate theater seats up there in the gallery, measly tickets for the circus, which stank of horse dung. I was always paid in pennies for the lessons I taught. My whole existence is a long, narrow chain, linked together with pennies. With my last penny and for the last time I will pay for a woman, everything that I've seen in hot dreams at night. One last moldy penny will be added to the end of the chain and . . . my final account will be settled.

◆

## 11TH OF TISHRE

Yesterday was a day of paltry experiences and vivid impressions.

It was Yom Kippur. Jews, weak from fasting, wandered to and fro like shadows over the pavements, between one prayer and the next, hoarse from spouting too much *makhzer*. Jews fasted, welcoming the hardship of fasting with love, with pale, taut faces, and with submission. In the meantime each had a little something to sniff—either tobacco, or "drops" from bottles—for refreshment. They enjoyed themselves and shook their heads with vigor. The Yom Kippur holiday fast seemed to affect even the walls, the bridge, and the small patches of sky overhead. The buildings themselves stood holy and pale with a weary smile, listening through spotless windowpanes to the songs and prayers streaming from every direction.

This was all just in the Jewish streets; beyond those streets and alleyways, lustful life simmered as always. Carriages circulated, making a furious clamor, and people, as though making bets on who could overtake whom, rushed and flew at breakneck speed, against, past, behind each other. Like yesterday and the day before, the polished windowpanes of expensive shops gleamed, and, smiling with the eternal smile of cold, smooth glass, they waved in all directions, tickling curious eyes, hypnotizing passersby into forgetting for a moment that they were in a hurry, causing them to stop and gaze at all the wondrous goods, sparkling behind the glass . . .

I'd gone to bed late the night before. I awoke, somewhat drowsy from the fat *kapore* chicken I'd eaten the previous evening, and I looked at the clock: it was already midday.

An odd, latent feeling inside me—weak and beautiful, like the dying echoes of childhood—drove me to the synagogue.

But when I got there, they wouldn't let me in because I hadn't thought to buy a ticket in advance for the High Holidays. So I stood in the street and listened. The cantor sang, the choir boys joined in; women read *tkhines* and cried. Apparently they were struck by thoughts of mortality. *Ha. They're all sighing. What do they have to sigh about? Do they care that I'm going to blow my skull open? They need to make a living, that's what they care about.*

And suddenly I lit up in anger against myself: *Do I need money? Health? A long life? What am I standing here for? Am I angry? Why do my lips let through a smile without my consent?*

I set off toward cleaner streets that roared hungrily and were, as always, full of noise, where there wasn't even a hint of fasting or prayer.

Hastily, my heart raging as if in search of revenge, I wandered from café to café, from restaurant to restaurant, unable to calm down.

The Christian restaurateurs famously wonder about this strange holiday, when all the Jews are allowed to eat *treyf*. And now, that long-awaited holiday had arrived. The restaurateurs beamed with pleasure, scrambling forward and bowing to each guest with a smile. The place was full of young Jews, eating and drinking, smoking and playing chess or checkers, casting suspicious glances at the door, which tinkled whenever it opened or closed . . .

I found myself a corner, sat down, and ordered a drink, trying not to stand out so I wouldn't be obligated to talk to the acquaintances I'd recognized among the crowd. One of them spotted me anyway and approached me, waving. He greeted me in high spirits: "How much kishke and coffee have you had today?" But I interrupted him emphatically, saying that my head hurt and asking him to leave me in peace.

Waiters in white aprons, with respectable easy gaits, served me. They brought everything I asked for with saccharine humility. In the end, when I ordered the cutlet *à la marchal* with wine, they became so doting that it nauseated me, and I lost my appetite.

I have always hated the race of waiters. They divide the world into two types of people: good, decent people who leave tips of twenty kopecks, and bad, petty people who leave less, or nothing at all. I've always hated their excessive subservience, their feigned stupidity, their cheap smiles. You order something politely—they smile. You show your temper when they forget something—they smile again. You laugh at their clumsiness, or their apron, and the familiar grin stays irrevocably fused to their face. Especially yesterday, I was sick to my bones of them. Their presence disheartened me. And so, to spite them, in revenge for their greed, I left nothing behind, letting them know that I was not the "gentleman" they called me. The waiters cleared my table with open malice. One of them even cursed me behind my back, and I was pleased to have provoked his wrath.

Of course, I've bought myself many little enemies for the few dozen kopecks that I've failed to distribute as the custom warrants. They will do as enemies when there are no other enemies to be had.

But in one café I suddenly had the urge to turn one waiter into a faithful friend. Finishing one last cup of coffee, unable to stomach another drop, I called the waiter over and placed a coin straight into his hand.

"Thirty kopecks in the till and five rubles for you," I said.

He stumbled and began to stammer, patting his apron, jingling the coins in his wide leather pocket. His hands were shaking.

I attempted to leave but he stood in my way.

"Don't you understand simple Russian?" I asked, smiling politely.

Then something happened that I hadn't expected. The eyes in that long face of his were damp, and he started to blink. Suddenly, gracelessly, he bowed and grabbed my hand, intending to kiss it. I shuddered, red in the face. I whispered to him bitterly: "Get away from me."

And I left.

I could feel many curious eyes on my back.

◆

From the right distance, in the city gardens, everything still looks green and fresh. But as you approach and look closer at the trees, you see yellow, withered leaves along with the green. Here and there they steal onto the branches like a contagious infection whose first symptoms are barely noticeable, but whose end is bitter . . . The foulness had crept into the branches and was waiting patiently, with a confident, yellow smirk, with a veiled contempt for all that's green and healthy.

There's an unpleasant humidity in the air, and the faint scent of mold. It's a smell that announces that autumn is on the way. Anyone who walks in the gardens is only deluding themselves that it's still summer and that autumn is still far off. That's why they are all dressed in summer clothes and wearing straw hats, to show that it's true. But their movements suggest a hint of autumn, a hidden, quiet worry peeking out of their eyes. I can read their minds: autumn ... rain ... sadness ... winter ... warm clothes ... a warm apartment ...

That living, natural décor suited my mood perfectly. I thought to myself: if they look at me, they'll imagine that I drink, walk, and observe. In short: that I'm a person like any other. But, what's this? What have I decided, eh? What's this heavy, shiny thing sleeping here in my pocket? Ah, sleep, my pretty!

There is a special chair set up in the gardens that offers to *"weigh each person for only ten kopecks."* Not having anything to do, I had myself weighed.

The man standing next to the balance-pan handed me a thin card with printed numbers: *"118 pounds 3 ounces."*

The card trembled in my hand. I walked around, touching the letters, looking at it again and again. I smiled to myself. Is it not pathetic? Here I am, a man who walks and moves and hears and sees. A man who understands and observes and reads and who's been perhaps overly preoccupied with the idea of the "superman"; I am, you understand, a man ... Twenty years I've suffered, and I suffer still and am desperate and preparing to commit suicide. And all of this adds up to only 118 pounds and 3 ounces! There you have it, 118, 3, you hear that? That measure includes the hands; the feet; the bowels that cry out when there's nothing to eat; the lungs that breathe; the brain that thinks. All my ideas, all my moods and feelings, all my memories and hidden experiences—everything goes into the scales. That unhappy 118 pounds incorporates this small, sick little Shloymke, who sat on a bench at his father's big, lonely house dreaming his black little dreams. And in addition, the current twenty-year-old man, who is preparing ... well, let's just say, to shoot himself in the head.

There you have it, help yourself to 118 pounds 3 ounces!

And what is such a measly weight next to the stone and brick giants—the walls that rise up all around? Stone palaces stand here on both sides of the street, edifices weighing hundreds of thousands of pounds, millions of pounds . . . certainly. And those same heavy materials do not worry, do not suffer, do not run to give lessons, do not hate or love anything . . . You can take a hammer and smash down a whole wall weighing many many pounds, and it won't feel a thing. It will only cause the dust to rise. But just try hacking off half a human arm, from me, for example, weighing only a few ounces . . . oh!

A medium-sized stone lay on the ground . . . I'd swear it weighed no more than my head. And yet, the stone, and my head: what a contrast! My head thinks and remembers and strives . . . and yearns. The stone—nothing. It lies there and that's all, the beggar! And both of them seem to weigh the same . . . no it's not quite so, and yet, how strange it is.

My head began to spin, and such neurotic thoughts made me ill. Oh, I can't stand these thoughts! Foolish and stubborn, they plague me unrelentingly, and I cannot be rid of them.

To clear my head, I started walking at a brisk pace, and began teasing myself.

"Make way, make way, here come 118 pounds, 3 ounces, in the form of a human. With hands and head and feet—just as sure as today is Yom Kippur!—118 pounds, 3 ounces, with a loaded revolver in his pocket. Make way, pardon me!"

I was still disturbed yesterday as I exited the gardens, bizarre thoughts scrambling through my head like ants in their nest. The sun went down. The day perished, the western sky glowing sickly red as it took its final breath. A strong breeze blew, pausing every now and then. The humidity in the air started to feel heavier, announcing autumn hiding just around the corner. Once again I returned to the Jewish quarter, where they had just finished the *mayrev* prayers. Minyans, synagogues, and prayer houses opened their rectangular mouths and with hot, musty air, started spitting out thousands of Jews—men, women, and children. Everyone was rushing home to appease their stomachs. Blessing and kissing each other hurriedly for the sake of the mitzvah, the streets came alive.

I stood there for quite some time, separated, alone, on the corner of a narrow alleyway, enduring the pushing and shoving of knees and elbows, courtesy of the hungry passersby. I stood and observed the great masses, snaking on all sides through the gray evening, and I was besieged by negative thoughts. I all but gnashed my teeth. Who was I so angry with? What in God's name did I want?

I thought: here is a large community of thousands of people, each one a heart unto itself, a world of its own; they all love themselves and protect their own little bodies with all their feeble might and meager talents. And they only weigh ... each world with all its hopes and goals ... a couple of hundred pounds, a few miserable pounds. But wait! You only have to wait a few decades, six or seven at most, and all those pounds of uneasy material will be dead. Walking through here sincerely believing that they are "humans" ... They will be erased from the world and will rot. Unruly weeds will take pleasure in their juices. And the clothes and ties and silken garbs they dress up in, showing off and boasting will become rags, and the rags will become dust. And the dust will be blown away by the wind. Crazy pounds of flesh! These very streets you walk on, these buildings and walls you live in, will be obliterated, and new ones will be built in their place, in a different configuration, with a new style, and not a trace of you will be left. You're wishing each other a good year, are you? Really? A good year?

But the crowds of Jews apparently had no idea what I was thinking about them. They were rushing home. And written on each one's face: food, food, food.

# CHAPTER 4

## THE 14TH OF TISHRE

So, what is happening? Have I forgotten? Why have I not settled my "final account," as I call it? The Devil knows. Twice already, I've set off to *that* place, but as soon as I reach the winding, sloping alleyway and see the red lantern swimming out of the darkness I lose my nerve; an inexplicable dread befalls me, and I turn around and come back . . .

This will not do! It is weakness, weakness pure and simple.

What is even more surprising is that the affections I feel toward my revolver seem to have cooled somewhat. I can now go whole days without looking at it, and no longer spend whole nights caressing it, alone in my room with the lamp burning. I am not sleeping well and when I wake up my brain is as blank and dark as the cellars of a ruin. I rise in the morning, drink tea without appetite, and head out to my lessons with mechanical punctuality. I teach my students and correct their mistakes, sneaking a glance, every now and then, at my pocket watch. Though, frankly, I have no reason to hurry. Who's waiting for me? Where do I need to go? I no longer shout nervously at my students when they forget their homework and I've stopped praising them when they give a correct answer, even when they excel. They steal artless glances at me during the lessons, with childish curiosity and a hidden, infantile suspicion. Their young eyes seek in my stony face the explanation for the change they've noticed in me. I don't like how they stare at me. It makes me uncomfortable; I feel as though I'm wrapped in spiderwebs, unable to move freely, and all I can do is frown at them. When I can stand it no more I croak at them: "Don't stare at my nose; you'll find nothing there. Look at your books instead!"

I have three new students lined up, found for me by some acquaintances, at a very good rate: fifteen rubles a lesson! I've never been paid that much before. I'm due to begin teaching during the week of Sukkes. The question came to me in passing, *What do I need the lessons for anyway? Why now? Now that I've almost finished with . . . I can't fathom it. Why did I accept them. And why now of all times have the rich families taken a liking to me? Is this any time for them to start offering me work? What a strange world!*

Even reading, my only solace up to now, no longer brings me any pleasure. I'm so sick of all the books I could vomit. As soon as I open one I feel like I've long known its contents, everything inside is old and outdated: old rags, piles of old rags rebound in colorful new ribbons. I'll put aside the book with a yawn, clear my throat, lie down on the sofa and stare at the ceiling; I stare at it as if there were something to see. But the ceiling is also old and familiar in every detail, from the dirty corner to the white stain on the right, to the black point on the left, next to the wardrobe: the body of a dead fly, which had become wedged there and dried out.

This evening, overcome with loathing toward my room, the furniture, and the noise in the streets, I decided to go to the theater. *Faust* was playing, the opera I used to love so much, which I've heard and seen so many times without ever being able to sate my appetite. But this time, as soon as the red Mephisto appeared on stage and began to sing, it was clear to me that I detested him from the bottom of my heart. I asked myself: *How can you go and watch something you've seen so many times already?*

I left.

I've stopped paying visits to my acquaintances. I know that I'd only have to look at the same furniture and pictures I've seen before, those same all-too-familiar faces, and listen to the same conversations, those mundane pleasantries I've heard countless times.

The idea of drinking, on the other hand, suddenly seems very appealing.

I'm drawn to the prospect of going into a dingy tavern, for example—it has to be dingy: the air filled with the fug of alcohol fumes and tobacco smoke—and drinking till I'm blind drunk, drinking until the walls and people and tables and glasses blur into one fluid mixture, with me right there in the middle, a hearty, drunken smile on my face.

But I hold myself back with all my force. I'm afraid that it may weaken my resolve. I'm afraid of the effect such a powerful substance might have on my will, causing it to burn up and go to pieces at the first hurdle. I intend to finish what I've started. No. I must die with a firm resolve, with all my willpower, and with a clear head. Do I not require a clear head to write my final will and testament— a farewell letter—according to the age-old custom of dying and suicide? I have nothing to say and no one to say it to. What should I write? Perhaps the banal, overused phrase: "I blame no one"? It's a lie: everyone is to blame for my suicide. Should I write, "I blame everyone for my death"? That too is a lie: no one is to blame. It would be better to leave behind just a little note, a single line on a thin strip of paper: "No one is to blame for my death and everyone is to blame." Ha ha! That would be more true than anything! But a little too original for those who will find the note after I'm gone, pawing at it with prying fingers and scrutinizing it from every angle. "A fine phrase!" they'll say, smiling ironically. But how could they possibly grasp the eternality, the infinity that I, the dying, feel within those words?

I need my clear reason for my own benefit. I must cross the threshold with conviction, without doubts—above all without doubts. The threshold between life and death is a narrow one, no wider than the shiny bullets lying ready in my revolver's skull. You just need the courage to press the right spot and you're already on the other side. The new horizon must be wide and clear, there can be no clouds there, for that is a beautiful death, a true death.

But what has happened? My resolve seems to have distanced itself from me, hiding under whole mountains of other thoughts and moods. I seem now to be estranged, both from life and from death . . . How can that be?

◆

### THE 16TH OF TISHRE

Eureka! . . . I've solved the riddle. I've found the key to my recent puzzlingly stagnant disposition.

I've weighed up my behavior, my character, temperament, and thought processes of late and compared them to my earlier life, my earlier moods and now I understand . . .

I realize that I've reached a dead zone between two equal forces, where even the strongest energy loses momentum. Life is pulling me from one side, death from the other and I hang between both magnets, spinning in one spot around my own axis—neither here nor there. I've pulled myself away from life, set out toward death but, being impractical in such matters, I've fallen into a point where the forces of life and death are equally far away, or equally close, and my will, the third force, is canceled out between the two . . . Now I live, drink, eat, sleep, and move only out of habit, out of pure inertia . . .

I've come to a place where, if I wish it I can die, just as I decided, or if I want, by all means, I could keep living . . . I would just have to sell the revolver, or destroy it and continue to live like the masses, who clutter the streets day in, day out.

The scales of life and death are in equilibrium for me now. Neither side is one jot heavier than the other, nor do they lean in any particular direction. Seeing as this colorless, lifeless state is likely to continue over many tedious days, it's up to me to try, with all my might, to tip the balance once and for all.

Black or white, but not gray. Cold or hot, but not tepid. To soar to the heavens or to plummet to the depths, but not to hover in one place.

What does life want from me? Why do the lanterns beckon me so at night? Why does the morning sun torment me with its rays of light? Why do the streets laugh so merrily? I don't want to go on. I can't go on. I've already given it much thought and have decided I must tip the balance in favor of death—things cannot continue as they are. To carry on living just for the sake of living? Live as I do now only in order to move my arms and legs and lug a head around on my shoulders?—I don't want to, I mustn't, I can't!

You have to grab hold of a situation like this and shake it, shake it till it makes waves that spread under their own steam; you want it to swerve and lurch about with abrupt ferocity, and ardor. Above all, it must happen quickly.

But how do I tip the scales in favor of death? It's simple:

(1) Cancel all my private lessons, spend the last of my money and be left without food or lodgings.

(2) Sell all my winter clothes, my fur, my gloves, and be left without a stitch to wear. Winter is on the way . . .

(3) Break off contact with all my acquaintances (I have no friends in any case). Break with them decisively, push them out if they try to visit. There should simply be nowhere for them to find a foothold.

A few more deeds such as these, and it won't be long before the *need* comes. The imperative will drop its heavy stone, tipping over the balance toward death.

In the past, these things would not have bothered me much—on the contrary, hunger and want made me feel superior to others—not anymore. Now I need a justification to satisfy my instinct for self-preservation. I have to prove that I'm bankrupt, bankrupt in every sense. I'm long dead in fact, I continue to live only because I have not yet been *there* . . .

Indeed, that's the only way I'll be able to close all doors, the doors that lead to life. Only one single, narrow path will be open to me: toward death!

Necessity will not allow me to tread water as I'm doing now; it will spur me on, compelling me to: go go go!

And wouldn't you know it, now of all times when I must take my pulse, listening intently to every beat so as not to be in any doubt, now of all times they offer me a couple of lucrative tutorials and I go and accept them! A pity.

Now of all times I have the chance to earn a whole hundred rubles a month, earning like I've never earned before. I could rent a nice apartment, dress well, buy new books, live comfortably, live with dignity . . .

But, I get it, the Devil is dancing around me. He's found himself some work, he intends to drag me back into the life that I've grown weary of. Aha, that's where he wants to drag me? Doing with me whatever he pleases? Offering me trinkets? No. Not this time. Tomorrow I'll begin canceling my lessons. Tomorrow! An end to students, new and old. Enough of students and parents and fifteen rubles—enough, enough! It's a wasted effort. Once I start it won't be difficult to take the second step and sell my worldly possessions, followed by the next step of breaking off all human contact; nothing will compel me to visit people, shake their hands, or chat with them . . .

Yes. I'll start tomorrow.

◆

### THE 17TH OF TISHRE

I begin . . .

I begin putting my decision into practice. I forcibly tip the balance toward death, emerging slowly from my unmoving, apathetic state. My heart beats faster, harder, my feet move more nimbly. My nervousness has returned, along with the kaleidoscope of ideas that spin and shift within me, turning black, turning white, drowning and swimming to the surface.

I had only to start the process for everything to continue under its own momentum. like a loose log on a mountain top: touch it with one finger and it will start to roll, faster and faster the further it goes, from that one piece of wood a living thing emerges, striving and pushing, leaping and making its way downward, downward.

That's how tightly wound my nerves were.

Dispassionately, I went to the homes of my employers with a gentle smile and a polite little bow of the head to cancel my lessons, the old ones as well as the new. Like a truly practical man I demanded the money that was already owed me, adding: "I'm afraid I really must go, no two ways about it . . . a pity . . . a real pity, but I have no choice but to give up teaching. Pardon me."

I caught my employers in the middle of their Sukkes time, holiday moods. Everything was spick and span in their homes, silverware and white tablecloths all around, their movements and conversations were also in keeping with the holiday spirit. Gentle and a little carefree. Today is something of a holiday for me too; in its honor I've dressed up in my best suit with a new paper collar. Today is the *Feast of Canceled Lessons*. My soul is brimming and a feminine tenderness flows through my veins.

I left the houses, satisfied, exercising my own free will. I was happy to be so good at playing the role of the man who must go out of town. For the first time in my life I felt I had control over myself and over my own destiny, free to decide what I'll do the following day. I decided, took the responsibility, and acted. Decided and acted. I decided to give up tutoring, and so I gave it up. That's how I like it.

But when I went to Herr Mikhl's today to quit my final lesson, something happened that I did not appreciate. Before I'd even had time to remove my hat, put down my cane and say, "Good morning," Madame Mikhl approached me—Madame Mikhl with her well-fed face, wrinkly and covered in powder, with her unplugged lips which cried out for respect, with her thin, red kaftan that accentuated her large bosoms—and with a salty sweetness admitted that she did not know which of us was to blame. Me, the teacher, or her son, the student. As it stood she saw no further need for my tutorage and so . . . she would pay me what I was owed for the month.

The elation I'd felt all day vanished in an instant, up in smoke. That lady stole it all with her respectable face and my ego suffered a heavy blow. It hurt that I'd been banished. I was on the verge of losing my temper. I wanted to thank Madame for saving me the trouble and explain that, actually, I'd come for that very reason myself. But in that same moment of shame and despondency, my hand slipped, of its own volition, into my pocket and brushed against the revolver . . . my anger melted away in an instant, dissipating like a light vapor in the sun.

A cold smile swam over my face: *What is there to be angry about? Ha ha! Does it not amount to the same thing? It's not worth a damn. Soon, in a couple of days . . .*

With a smile on my face I walked, for the last time, through the familiar door with its charming brass sign: "*Leo Mikhl— Merchant.*" Madame Mikhl watched me in disbelief. It turns out she'd wanted to see what sort of face a Jewish teacher makes when you dismiss him. She wanted to savor the moment, but it was not to be.

◆

## THE 18TH OF TISHRE

Canceling those lessons was a good start; my indifference vanished with remarkable speed. My appetite has returned, along with my desire to read. Last night, I slept deeply and long through the night. I have no more doubts. These are the positive results of my resolve. Yes. The balance is tipping over, further toward death. That's it: lower, lower! Soon it will reach the ground. But wait!

I must still pay a visit to *that place . . .*

Last night I slept particularly soundly. The book I was reading fell to the floor. I left the lamp burning and I sank into a thick, sweet slumber, the likes of which I haven't had in ages. I slept the pure sleep of the blessed; no hint of dull melancholy, no dreams, and no sudden awakenings. A slice of oblivion between one day and the next.

So this is how good they have it: those who don't know of restless nights, nights without repose, full of nightmares and winking shadows? Those cursed nights!

How much of my blood have they spoiled, how much brain matter have they caused to dry up? The fear of nights like those bleeds over into the daytime. You are certain in advance that you're not going to sleep and you try everything. You go out and walk and walk for hours through the streets and to the outskirts of the city until your knees start to tremble. To further ensure a good night's sleep you drink a glass of beer. Your head spins a little and as you undress you're sure that as soon as you climb into bed you'll drop off like a stone. But when you lie down the pillows become as hard and flat as a board, your legs grow too long and you can't for the life of you find enough space for them. The blanket becomes too hot and your skin burns up as in a fever; you throw the blanket aside but a nasty draft finds you and you start to shiver. Your eyes burn under your clenched brow. You close them tightly with that singular stubbornness of one who wants to sleep but cannot. You open your eyes and it's dark—dark in the room, dark in your heart. Your whole being is nothing more than a patch of darkness in the general gloom, eating away at you silently—an hour goes by, two hours, three ... the minutes draw themselves out as if from pitch. With an exhausting lethargy they drip; your nerves begin to bounce. The barking of a dog reaches your agitated ears, the creak of a far-off door, the jangle of a caretaker's keys, the dim whistle of a locomotive, and after the slightest movement, the lightest touch feels like glowing screws being driven into your skull.

And if you should be bitten by that thief-like parasite, the flea, you writhe as though bitten by a snake. If a shaft of light should enter from somewhere and move across the ceiling, it feels like you're being jabbed with needles. Everything in the darkness acquires a certain air of spiteful impudence, turning up their noses at you somehow . . . the furniture, the dishes, everything is looking at you, their entire will is bent only on tormenting you and keeping you awake. Your will, your consciousness lose their balance. You grind your teeth, you're angry and you don't know with whom. The ceramic tiles of the stove sparkle white in the darkness. *Damn your bones!* Though a stove does not generally have any bones. Your bed creaks. *May all beds suffer a bitter fate!* A hair comes loose and touches your nose just to spite you: *Down with all noses! Sitting there in the middle of faces like that, not letting anyone get a wink of sleep.*

And by the time you're utterly exhausted and you don't have the energy left to battle the great, dense night you begin to slumber a sparse, fragmented slumber, no less exhausting than the insomnia itself. And the next morning you feel as though you haven't slept at all. You experience that heavy, unpleasant sensation of a starving man who has filled his belly with water, tight as a drum, in order to still his hunger.

But last night I slept and slept and slept. Nothing disturbed me. I did not grind my teeth, did not bite the pillows and, when I awoke, I felt so light, ready to carry out the most arduous task in the world . . . it's enough to make you want to shoot yourself.

So I'm rid of the lessons, what's next? Time to finish with my acquaintances, begone with them! Time to sell everything I have, go to that house of ill repute and make use of my instrument. Listen to me, joking like this!

That's how it should be.

# CHAPTER 5

## THE 20TH OF TISHRE

Yesterday evening, at the midpoint of Sukkes, I came home so tired I wanted to jump straight into bed.

I entered my room only to find Mirkin on my bed, lying on top of the sheets. He was sound asleep, a slight snore fluttering through his narrow, pink nostrils. It seems he'd made himself comfortable while waiting for me to return, and had dozed off.

Mirkin is a fine-looking lad, jovial and strong. I consider him a mere acquaintance, but he's gotten it into his head that we are firm friends. He is attentive to my words but often finds them unsettling. In such moments he tries to lighten my heavy mood by inviting me to the theater—on him—or by buying us beer and something to eat.

All in all he is—how should I put it—a bit simple. He has a sensitive heart and is pained by the suffering of others. Essentially I don't like him—I don't like anybody—but when my nerves are on edge I enjoy venting my gall at him, all my bitter thoughts, safe in the knowledge that he'll take it all without protest, even when my words offend him. He'll weigh up my every sentence and will attempt to comfort me. And because he has pretensions of being a good friend, he often allows himself to call me a swine, or an idiot, and curse me to the Devil—he's overly fond of curses involving the Devil—but he'd be quite shocked if I were to roll up my sleeves and actually head to the Devil.

And there he was asleep on my bed, face up, with a mouth full of twinkling white teeth, so healthy they looked as though they could chomp through bone. A smile floated over his cherry-red lips, the youthful smile of one who takes pleasure in everything, even in an unplanned nap such as this. His stout, fleshy legs spreadeagled like scissors, his broad clean-shaven chin, his soft, blond hair, his youthful, downy moustache—it all came together in one beautiful harmony, a harmony of security and life force, flowing unperturbed like a mountain stream.

I stood there for a few moments regarding his familiar face with curious detachment. In sleep his face was motionless, could not hide from my penetrating gaze. Sleep had paralyzed his features, serving them up before my eyes so that I could observe them to my heart's content.

A nebulous sort of hatred arose inside me, pushing me forward. Slowly, almost reflexively, I turned to look in the mirror: a skinny, exhausted visage; sparse, colorless hair—neither ash-colored, nor brown, nor blond; a large bony nose with a red abscess, which had settled in on the very tip, with no intention of budging; beady, sunken eyes, tired and dull.

That was my face.

I compared the image in the mirror with the sleeping face on the bed, and I shuddered. I'd never felt so loathsome, so gaunt, so pitiful as I did in that moment. My nose had never protruded so awkwardly as it did right then.

The sleeping man smiled triumphantly; it seemed that even in sleep, he felt my strange, misplaced hatred and took pleasure in it, a hidden scorn floating in his snores.

I could feel that, any minute now, I might find myself raising my hand to slap him full force in his smug face, covering that quiet, sleeping smile in blood. But I suppressed this wicked instinct and deliberately caught my foot in the leg of the chair, knocking it over and making a racket.

Mirkin awoke with a deep intake of air, startled and confused, opening his eyes wide. It took a moment for him to find his tongue and let out a sound from his cherry lips.

"Aha, you're back?"

I hid my pallid countenance from him and replied, "Here I am . . . sorry, did I wake you? I tripped on the chair as I came in."

And in my heart I thought: *The Devil take him, coming in here and having a lie down on my bed.*

He was awake now and in the mood for chatting. What can you say? I'm sure after my death he'll still be the same Mirkin as before, the very same.

He rubbed his eyes vigorously, wiping away the last traces of sleep with his strong white hands, and said, "It's a habit of mine. I can't sit idle. Either I eat, or drink or read or go for a walk, or . . . you know yourself . . . but, yeah, as soon as I have nothing to do, I fall asleep. Yes, yes—"

The final "yes" came out together with a long yawn accompanied by a smile.

I said nothing.

After the yawn, which appeared to give him as much enjoyment as his nap, he brought his face in order and asked:

"You don't have a cigarette do you? I've run out."

"Firstly," I answered coldly, "you know I don't smoke, and secondly, I don't have any."

"Ah, you idiot, why don't you smoke? It's a great thing, smoking, I'm telling you."

He paused.

"You don't smoke because you're worried about your health, is that it?"

I smiled mutely. I tried to hold back the smile but my lips had a life of their own.

*A few days before I shoot myself in the head, and he thinks I'm worried about my health!*

"Hey, why so quiet?" Mirkin continued. "Do you have anything to read? I couldn't find any of your books earlier."

"I took them all back to the library, and sold the others."

Mirkin sensed that there was something I wasn't telling him. A month had passed since we'd last paid each other a visit, or spoken a word to each other apart from the occasional "Good morning" in passing on the street. I'd been too busy with my revolver. Now he must have sensed the animosity in me, sensed that I was not my usual self. In the half-gloom I could feel him scrutinizing me with a long, clear, questioning look: an expression only his big blue, suspicious eyes are capable of. The satisfaction vanished from his lips.

I responded with a sideways glance and held my tongue. An ominous silence had crept in, a silence tinged with suspicion. My nerves couldn't take it, and an anger started to build up inside me.

*What does he want from me?*

"You know, Mirkin," I said abruptly, "that you're an ignoramus, don't you?"

I said it with a smile, with languid venom. I was sure he'd take offense and tell me to go to the Devil, but he said nothing, just looked at me like before.

I could imagine that, just then, a curtain between us would part and something hidden would be revealed. My voice on the verge of faltering, I asked:

"Should I light the lamp?"

He laughed.

"Since when are you afraid of a few shadows?"

He stood up, approached me and placed a pale hand on my scrawny shoulder.

"Tell me, swine, what's wrong with you? You're so distant and pale. You're lonely; that's it, isn't it? Are you sure you don't want to come with me to the brothel? You're a fine lad, no question. You'll make something of yourself. Come on, let's go to a dance lesson; I'll teach you the art of dancing. What do you say?"

I laughed madly, but succeeded in tempering it so as not to appear quite so frantic. I thought to myself: *Good, good, dancing. Let's dance in honor of the revolver, let's dance in honor of the Angel of Death!*

Mirkin was satisfied that he'd made me laugh so heartily, and continued speaking in the dark:

"You know, I'm a great lover of dance. Dancing intoxicates me. Music, even more so. Sometimes when I'm sitting by myself reading, I'll suddenly hear an organ-grinder playing in the yard, playing a *Kamarinskaya*, or a *Kekuak*, or a *Matsesh*, I'll grab a chair, imagine it's a girl, and I'll start dancing in time with the music—like this, you see?" (he grabbed a chair and off he went dancing). "One, two, three . . . One, two, three . . ."

He forgot what he'd begun, got all fired up and off he went, babbling away about all the different types of dances that he had or had not mastered, about beautiful, passionate melodies, all the while spiritedly wagging his tongue.

He talked about how the girls love to dance with him, they'd do anything for a dance with him . . . "I spin them around so quickly they get dizzy and abandon their warm bodies into my arms: there you go! There's a waist for you, there's a breast, so close you can feel their quick breaths on your face ... once I almost died from the thrill of it: a long cool braid of hair, so smooth and black, came undone and wrapped itself around my neck in the middle of the dance ... oh!"

I felt like saying something to offend him, to puncture his childish joy, the joy of one who has never suffered, never furrowed his brow. But I had no harsh words ready, so instead I said what had been waiting on the tip of my tongue, so cold and still:

"You know that you're going to die, don't you?"

"What do you mean, die?" Mirkin said, becoming subdued.

"Has it never occurred to you?" I asked in my cryptic voice. "You know what *die* means don't you? A soldier is walking past, he drops his gun by mistake, it goes off—you die! It's raining, you slip, onto the tracks of an oncoming tram and—you die! ..."

"You die," Mirkin repeated after me, like an echo before trailing off.

The heavy atmosphere had passed, aided by the general stillness of the room.

"You know?" Mirkin said a moment later, his voice muffled now.

"What?"

"When you pronounce the word *die* it sounds different than when other people say it. It would not have bothered me if someone else had said it."

Pause. A minute later.

"But what made you suddenly think about death? Yes one day I'll die, of course I will, but as long as I'm still alive I need to live. Live it up until the very last spark. Take everything, everything, to the Devil!"

*Aha*, I thought, *It's come to this already, just you wait!*

He was ready to pick up the chair and start dancing again, perhaps to drive away the feeling of dread that was now building up in the room, but my face and my cold voice demanded he stay right where he was.

"Yes, to live, to take everything from life, I know. All those hackneyed platitudes of people who are afraid of themselves. But know this! There is a whole lot of natural evil in the world, and only a small amount of good. The good is also artificial: it's man-made. And what little good there is is sparingly, very sparingly distributed. Each person only gets a tiny glob of it on the end of his knife. The sly people in their petty short-sightedness strive to use their meager portion of goodness piece by piece. Every day they lick off another drop, every day—a drop. To make life's tiny intoxicating pleasures last, in order to have a little something to enjoy each day until the last moment . . . Their bovine instinct warns them that if they use up their whole allotment of goodness in one go, they'll suddenly be left with a dark, empty space over their tiny worlds, and they will never again have anything to fill it with, save perhaps with mere yawns, you understand? You'll be fine, Mirkin, if you live like those people. If you make do, day to day, with just a little goodness, just a modicum of happiness. With modest strivings—God forbid you should rock the boat—then you'll always be satisfied, you and your soul. You'll be around a long time, you'll endure and not be bored. You'll work by day, you'll sleep at night. During the day you'll have lunch and in the evening you'll drink tea and read the newspaper. When the time comes to get married, you'll find a match. You shouldn't marry without a dowry. You'll be content and your parents will be happy. You'll buy furniture and you'll have a kitchen and a bedroom. Every Saturday, you'll entertain guests and you'll have children with clean clothes and brushed hair. That's how *you'll* live, you'll live I'm telling you . . . but there are others, such as Ecclesiastes, the Epicureans, the Karamazovs, they are naïve, they don't understand how one can be content scrupulously sipping one's portion of goodness, drop by drop. They cannot fathom how one can withhold a great passion, like a dog on a chain, being thrown leftovers . . . like children they cannot hold back and so they drink up all the goodness, thirstily, in one gulp. And do you know what happens to such people? Boredom, despair, disgust toward others, and toward everything they see and hear. Once all the goodness has been swallowed up everything is suddenly empty, everything loses its color. Then you grab yourself by the head, rubbing your eyes nervously and you observe everything with hatred: *This* is life? And we expected happiness? And we expected the Messiah to come?"

As far as I could make out by the gray light from the window, Mirkin had no idea what I was talking about. He made every effort to feign the earnest expression of one who understands another. The whole time I was speaking he furrowed his brow, until his face ached, nodding his head like a horse with a nasty fly on its back, whose tail is too short to whack it. I walked over to him silently, secure in the power of my words. With careful, secretive footsteps I went up to him like a cat stalking a mouse in the darkness. I felt like sinking my nails into his skin, deep, deep, until I drew blood.

Night was slowly falling; in my vision Mirkin and the bed he sat on began to blend into one another, into one fantastic piece of darkness. I touched his shoulder, and he trembled. I knew that he would.

"But let's say that you *must* live, or that you live for the sake of the process of living itself, without a clear sense of purpose, without a sure path, without any real consciousness. You simply *have* to exist! But what about old age? Have you, young, healthy, able fellow that you are ever thought about that?—Old age!

"Have you ever imagined how you're going to rot alive, physically and mentally, and no one will even notice? Have you ever considered the ugliness of the decaying persistence which comes with old age? Have you pictured a mouth with false teeth, a brain with false thoughts? Have you pictured eyes without eyebrows and skinny crooked bones instead of legs? Or shaky, gnarled hands, the color of earth?

"Your proud chest will cave in—who will want to press themselves against it then? Your face will wither, blue sacks will form under your eyes—who will want to kiss it? Your heart, worn out like a rag, no one will want to sow anything there. And if one *were* to plant something, would anything grow? Desire is no desire anymore, feeling, no feelings and you watch through dull, old eyes as so many fresh, merry, carefree young people take your place, reigning over your world, coming along and treading mercilessly over everything you've ever held dear, driving you away from the stage of life with mockery, whistling and fanfare. Your pretty heart will nearly burst with envy, an old man's envy; you'll be filled with the old yearning, but you will have to hold your tongue and wait with hidden sighs and pains until it's time for you to expire once and for all.

"You hear that Mirkin? I feel that I, civilized European from the twentieth century, am beginning to understand the 'savage' custom of the Eskimos and Tunguskans in the distant north, out there in the unending tundras … do you know what they do, Mirkin? They kill their elders! Whenever someone grows old in their tribe—they kill him! You understand? They wrap him in a white bearskin and the next oldest in the tribe stabs him to death. They make a whole celebration of it, with dancing … they drink whole basins of fish oil by the flickering shine of the Northern Lights ... Oh I understand them now, you hear me? I understand ..."

Mirkin suddenly rose and laid a gentle hand on my shoulder, his voice wavered slightly in the dark.

"Listen, brother, I don't understand everything you're saying. You have something inside you, something you were born with. I don't understand it, but there's something strange about you. The Devil knows, your tone frightens me. It's one thing to discuss an idea, but not with a tone like that. When you talk like that it sounds as though you're planning to murder someone. Upon my word, may it go to the Viennese Devil! Light the lamp, for crying out loud. What was it you said? They kill their elders and drink fish oil by the shine of the Northern Lights ..."

I said nothing.

"Shall I get beer? I'll go and buy some ..."

"Do."

"Half a dozen?"

"Half a dozen."

"Let's have ourselves a few drinks, then."

Minutes later I once again heard Mirkin's heavy footsteps on the stairs and the clinking of bottles. I thought he'd run off and wasn't coming back; that's what I would have done in his position. I'd have gone out to buy beer, but once outside I'd have changed my mind and not returned—leave the philosopher alone with his fear. But Mirkin? Beer, he brings me. He brings me beer and is ready to listen to more unpleasantness ... dupe that he is!

We lit the lamp, set up a whole battery of beer bottles, and sat down to drink.

I drank eagerly and looked at Mirkin; he could not stand my agitated gaze and instead stared with apparent fascination at the head of his beer. It was quiet. The only sounds breaking the silence were the sipping of the brown alcohol and Mirkin's breathing, which was getting faster and hotter. The beer shone in the lamplight like clear amber, topped with a soft, silvery foam. Silver bubbles, barely perceptible to the ear, popped inside the glass: *pik—pik—pik*.

A fly, the last one left over from summer, a souvenir of the warm sun, which had been hiding somewhere in the darkness, sensed that we'd lit the lamp and came out to warm itself by the flame. The fly's movements were sluggish, its transparent wings had no life left in them; it dragged its thin, emaciated legs behind it. Climbing up onto the lamp, it attempted to reach the glowing glass, and burned itself. It tried to open its wings to fly away, but could not; with all its energy it succeeded only in falling onto the table, belly in the air, legs flailing.

*zzzv . . . zzzv . . .*

"You see that?" I pointed at the fly, turning to Mirkin who had gone pale. "There you have it: autumn . . . desperation . . . misery, misery . . . ha ha!"

Mirkin shuddered. He grabbed the fly, flung it down under the table, and stomped with hatred on the cold hard floor, grumbling his habitual curse:

"The Devil take it!"

"What did you do that for? I asked with a laugh. "Why did you throw that poor old fly under the table? What's the problem, why shouldn't it warm itself?"

"Oh, give me a break . . . it's vile . . . a winged creature transformed into a worm . . . crawling, crawling . . . what does it have to complain about? *zzzv zzzv,* damn its eyes!"

"Yes," I said, already feeling somewhat drunk. "Yes, and one day you'll be just like it. Do you not feel your years already? I, for example, always feel the winter as soon as summer has begun. While others have a mind to greet the bright summer days with straw hats and decolté, I'm already worrying about the autumn muds, about snow and blizzards howling down the chimneys: *oooh oooh . . .* they'll come in the end. A month, a week, but they're coming, they must. I'm still young and yet I feel old age, it's lurking inside me, right here in my head, in my limbs . . . and here in my chest. I know it, it's waiting, mocking me. It's the same for you, but you don't feel it . . . Why not? Do you know? I'll tell you: It's because you're a tram horse. You've got a pair of blinkers on you and you watch the rails and pull . . . you inherited it from your forefathers. As they went to their graves they left the blinkers to you: here, wear these and be a good horse . . . watch you don't lose them, mind, otherwise you'll find yourself in an early grave. What were we talking about? Oh yes, we were talking about the fly. You threw it down under the table? Well the same will happen to you . . . I can already see it clear as day. You'll be cast aside; what use is your decrepit old carcass to anyone? You said it yourself: *zzzv zzzv tfu*—didn't you? Ha ha ha . . ."

Mirkin could not sit still. His face was drained of color, his eyes bulged.

"Listen," he shouted, "you're drunk, I swear you're drunk! You think this is funny? Why are you saying such strange things?"

I laughed bitterly.

"You think that's strange? Sit down and listen, I'll tell you something strange. When I was a boy and the teacher beat me for some trivial infraction, a terrible suspicion surfaced in my heart: I began to suspect that everyone I saw around me in my daily life, including my father, my stepmother, my uncle and aunt, my friends from *kheyder* and the teacher himself—I began to suspect that none of them were real people. No. Not people as they pretended to be, but demons; a host of wicked demons who'd disguised themselves as people. While I alone was the only real person in the world.

"The demons torment me, dressing up as teachers and fathers to torture me. That's why God sent me down among them . . . Look, I used to think to myself as I watched the teacher stroke his beard, or my father eat his lunch, or my stepmother snore . . . they're playing dumb. The more I tried to dispel my paranoia, the more it gnawed at me, leaving me no peace. I was convinced that all the mitzvahs and all the laws, all the respect and moralizing, the learning with the teacher—it was all created for my benefit, weak little me who was incapable of abiding by it. The evil spirits all around me had made it all up, just to have an excuse to reprimand me when I inevitably failed. To beat me, teach me to be a man, torment me. They're so cunning, those demons, that they also disguise themselves as little boys, who are beaten too, just as I'm beaten, so that I wouldn't suspect a thing . . . But I'm not so easily fooled . . . oh I won't be fooled . . .

"The strange suspicion stayed with me, sometimes dormant, sometimes keeping me awake at night. I did not speak about it to another soul. A shadow of that suspicion still falls on me from time to time even now. How do I know, for example, that you're really a human like me, and not a demon? Looks to me like you've disguised yourself in such a handsome, jolly face, in a strong human body only to excite lonely, ugly old me. Why did I knock over that chair earlier, eh? You don't know. You'll never know . . . tell me: who are you really? Ha ha! Maybe you're drinking beer with me, but the darkness is hiding the fact that you're sticking out a long, red demon-tongue at me? Tell me . . ."

"Cut it out," Mirkin sprang up again. "Cut it out, you madman ... I'll knock this table right over, bottles and all, you hear me?"

And then his voice went weak and his eyes regained their kindly shine, his pale hands gripping my arm.

"Please stop. I don't like it, I really don't. Don't be crazy ... the Devil take you!"

That stopped me short. I felt something cold melting in my heart, a sentiment bubbling and fermenting along with the beer-fog in my head. Mirkin's femininity passed over to me; my will became blurred. I suddenly felt a wave of self-pity. The cool smile was wiped from my face. On the verge of tears, I felt a need to say something, to complain to anyone willing to listen, willing to understand. Even great people feel the need to pour out their hearts to lesser people, for whom they have not a shred of respect.

"I assure you," I began, "I'm not crazy. Everything I've been saying up to now, I've been saying to myself, you understand? To myself ... I'm a strange one, is that how I seem to you? Could be. And do you know why? Because there is a great chasm between us: you possess a handsome shell, a handsome face, a slim body, a proud strut, a charming voice, life demands these things. It needs them, for such treasures life will lay itself down before you. What does it matter what's inside? You'll live, secure in your outer virtues, and God willing, you'll succeed, go with what you have and be happy. I will only accompany you with my long gaze, I'll stay here frozen in one place, or ... you know why? Because I don't have what you have, I have only a pile of nerves and a lump of red flesh, convulsing and boiling, with fervor and pain—they call it a heart. I have an all too sharp mind; ideas flash through me like lightning. But I don't have an outer skin to hide it all under, to protect it like a shell so that no one can see. Nobody must know what's under the shell. Have you ever in your life seen a fruit grow, ripen and become sweet without having a skin?

"Look at me and tell me who can I turn to with this scrawny, ugly face, with these weak hands, and this sickly body; with so many nerves and so little faith, with so many urges and dreams and so little hope to achieve them? What profession could I join. What do I have to offer the world, and what's in it for me? You see?"

A bitter taste rose in my throat. One glass of beer and I'd found my tongue. Mirkin looked at me with a compassionate curiosity. *There he is, about to cry from pity or laugh with relief that he's not like me.*

"Here's a declaration for you, if you still don't quite get it," I continued, unable now to hold myself back. I knew I was going too far, but I pressed on.

"When my father died, my uncles and aunts came together to dole out advice about what should be done with me. To whom should they sell my scrawny body into servitude? One suggested making a furrier of me. Another announced that evidently I could only find happiness as a goldsmith. A third, poking the table with his finger said there was nothing else for it but to send me off to be a watchmaker, a fine profession, a noble profession and a good way of putting bread on the table.

"And so I was sent off to become a watchmaker.

"You need patience for that kind of work: putting together the tiniest wheels, slowly adjusting the mainspring, removing and polishing each screw one by one, carefully, calmly. I lacked all of that. I didn't even manage to fix the old clock they gave me to practice on. I would pull the innards with a bent piece of wire to make it go faster. When my master left the room and the clocks would poke out their tin pendulums from the walls, ticking and tocking, I would become incorrigible. I had the feeling they were teasing me, preventing me from thinking. 'It's time to go home, *tick—tock*! At the market I saw gooseberries, *tack—tack*! My uncle says that, God willing, I'll earn my bread, *teck—teck*!

"I was filled with the urge to break every clock but one, and dance on the broken cogs. Down off the walls, down off the walls! To calm myself I'd set all the hands to the same hour, and drag them by their chains so they'd all chime at the same moment. There'd be a ringing and a striking in every language, every voice imaginable, soprano, baritone, and bass—but eventually the boss found out and I got what was coming to me.

"And so they sent me to a goldsmith. The workshop was full of soot and oil; dust and grease. It didn't take long for them to kick me out of there too.

"And so they tried out the advice of the third uncle and I became a furrier. The terrible stench of the pelts and collars and furs lingered in my head. I constantly felt like retching. In the evenings, when I would head home dejected, it seemed as though the whole world stank of fur, even the bread I ate, the tea I drank, the books I read and the bed I slept in . . . I used so much soap before eating or before bed, but it was no use. It felt like the whole world was pushing me with a wall of stench, trying to drive me once and for all to consumption. But I wouldn't allow myself to be tormented like that! One time my boss gave me a Kamchatka collar to smear with acid and nail to the stretching board. As soon as I took the nails in my hand the terrible acrid smell slapped me in the head, almost knocking me down. I imagined there could not possibly be anyone in the world who needed such a stinking fur. Surely, my boss too needed it like a hole in the head? His intent was nothing more than to cause me pain. He works here only to deceive me . . . he dreamed up this job only to torture me, me of all people: There you go, I hope you choke on it! Aha, so it's the same old demons again!—a wave of anger suffocated me, tears almost welled up in my eyes. Then I grabbed the acid, poured it out onto the soft, shiny hair, on the other side of the pelt. I beat it and piercing holes in it, with what joy I pierced it! And then . . . I ran away.

"Eventually my guardians had enough of me, *shlimazl* that I am. So they gave me what was left of the money from my father's inheritance and, at the age of sixteen, I left the town where I was born and unsuccessfully raised.

"Wandering from city to city, and from town to town. It wasn't long before my money ran out. And I began to go hungry and to study in earnest. My studies followed a strict curriculum, my hunger on the other hand, was unstructured, without beginning or end. I began to suspect that my lungs were not as healthy as they should be. I became convinced that my expenses were greater than my income, so to speak. The effort I was expending was worth more than the intellectual nourishment, and the materials I was cramming into my tired brain. I quit my studies—an end to learning! How do you put it?—to the Devil!

"I'm well acquainted with those half-dead students—I know the type. They emerge from the *yeshivas* and from dark corners of their small-town parents' houses, seeking a '*goal*.' They set off for the big cities, starve and languish in cellars, begging and earning a pittance from private lessons. They in turn take lessons from other students for next to nothing. Their brief youths stifled among dusty books, of no use to anyone. And by the time they've attained their goals they are already sick, depressed, and broken for good. Consumptive, short-sighted, emaciated, with protruding Adam's apples. I can't stand those sickly, talentless scholars with their pure diplomas, with their sunken chests, without flesh, without life. I can't stand those victims of education. They are nothing more than *yeshiva* boys in a new format. Eunuchs with feeble bodies, with thin noses, with blue spectacles and sunken eyes, gazing right into the grave.

"They hold life now in their ailing hands, they befoul the earth, infecting the air with their breath. Skeletons, the lot of them—skeleton doctors, skeleton philosophers, skeletons adept at mathematics, skeleton lawyers . . . I always picture them as large barrels with bits of brains, lumbering over the world high up on their thin fly legs . . . they walk around shaking. They fall down and right themselves, and they believe that life with all its airy cheer is made entirely for their benefit . . . Believe me, Mirkin, I too could reach the goals of those unhappy creatures, perhaps even surpass them, but I hate them as they are *now* with their petty small-mindedness and stinginess, with their eating bread with salt, lingering in cellars, and dreaming about their *future* careers.

"It's better that someone who has a chance of being happy with his youth, his strength, his own soul should learn—not me—even when he has achieved his goals.

"Someone who can learn for life's sake, rather than living for the sake of learning . . . But, listen . . ."

The word caught in my throat. I suddenly remembered what I'd decided . . .

*Why am I wasting my time talking to this imbecile? What do I care about teaching students? What do I want from him? Why am I philosophizing? Is that what's important? Is that what drove me to buy this thing that shines silently in my pocket? This needs to end now . . .*

Mirkin stood before me, his mouth slightly open. He was surprised by my abrupt silence.

"Listen," I addressed him in a weak, almost pleading voice, "get away from me!"

"Wha—at?" He was incredulous.

"Get out of here!" I said, louder this time, deliberately losing my temper. "I can't stand the sight of you, I'm sick of looking at you."

"You've lost your mind . . ." Mirkin gasped. But I didn't allow him to finish.

"Out!" I growled, all color draining from my face. "Did you not hear me?"

"So *that's* how it's going to be, is it? If so . . . really . . . the Devil take you, you beggar . . . the Devil take you and spit you out!"

"*Get out!*"

He started, looked at me like an animal, and ran off.

As the quick, frightened footsteps grew fainter on the stairs, I looked around, astonished. My drunkenness evaporated like smoke. It was midnight.

Had I really kicked out that fool just now? It seems I had. Simple. Before I was talking to him, telling him a few truths, a few lies, and then . . . I kicked him out.

Why?

For a trifle. A question! *Here, your excellency, is psychology, psychology, and psychology, and nothing more . . .*

Lost and alienated, I stood there for a while in the middle of my room. My head hung low. Then—I raised my hand and smacked my fist, as hard as I could, into my own temple.

*Shlimazl, what have you done?*

Meanwhile my hand slipped into my pocket and touched the revolver. I could swear it had moved against my will. The revolver was so warm! A cold, dull laugh burst out of my throat and hung in the air, in the nocturnal silence of the empty room.

With mystified terror I turned around to see where the laughter was coming from, so outlandish was the sound.

# CHAPTER 6

THE 22ND OF TISHRE

It appears I drank a little too much beer the other night, spilling out my guts and saying too much. Who was I speaking to? To Mirkin. Why was I speaking? Just like that, for no reason. Disgusting, disgusting.

I console myself with the fact that at least I didn't let anything slip about my revolver, or the box of bullets . . . No one must know about it, no one; mum's the word!

I can't contemplate the other night without shame. I'd felt the need for human sympathy, for pity—as I was lecturing Mirkin I noticed him preparing to take pity on me; he was almost there, but his sympathy fell away, and he showered me in rotten words.

If I hadn't spoken so much he would certainly have stood up, placed a warm hand on my shoulder, and consoled me, calmed me, pouring weak, clichéd, Mirkinesque consolation over me from his satisfied cherry lips, like the few pennies you'd throw to a beggar from a stuffed purse, like the moldy piece of bread a baker gives to a hungry man, but I could not tolerate such pity. Get out of my room, once and for all, get out! I'd said. And now my Mirkin is gone.

I no longer feel the dismal self-resentment I experienced just after kicking Mirkin out. I was merely protecting what was dear to me, guarding my death wish. I chased him away because he's a threat. He's a threat to me now, with his beer and his dancing and his gang of playboys and the charming girls he introduces to his acquaintances every chance he gets . . . Henia is one of his, after all, or used to be at any rate. He's dangerous. I've distanced myself from a danger. I'm left feeling like I've snuck up on a would-be attacker to get them before they get me.

But here's the thing: only one acquaintance remains, the most dangerous of all: Henia. Dear Henia—no one realizes just how dangerous she is! I have to be rid of her, just like Mirkin. If she came in here now, I'd command her to leave! But she won't come. A black cat has walked between us. It's been a month since I last saw her. I haven't visited since the wedding. She assumes I'm angry. I could go to her now and do something so abominable that she'll be left with no choice but to cast me out herself.

I have to end things with Henia tonight. Then I'll be free. Free with my will, free with my revolver. As a free man I'll set off to the whorehouse.

But how will I end things with her? What will I say to her? My hands are shaking.

It's a difficult operation, but I will go.

◆

## THE SAME DAY, EVENING

*Din—Din—Din* . . . the clock tower struck six in the evening. It was already dark. I counted the slow chimes with my eyes closed, then I remembered: Henia . . .

I felt at ease; just as if I were going to her for a quiet chat over a glass of tea with lemon. How pleasant it would be to see her pale face again, shining in the light steam of the samovar, turning so sadly cool.

I was calm and as I slipped on my coat I spoke to it like to a good friend. I slapped it like a connoisseur slaps a racehorse on the neck: "Well, well, my boy, tomorrow or the next day, we'll sell you, Reb Coat! You're still quite new though, eh? We'll sell you anyway, we'll sell you to the rag-and-bone man and then, Reb Coat . . ."

The pavements were crowded with restless people, cast in shadow, while the sky was filled with clear, unmoving stars, their golden brows twinkling with silent intelligence. I walked to Henia's place slowly, step by step, hands in my coat pockets, composed.

What choice did I have? At the same time the feelings awoke in me that always surface in such melancholy calm. I thought to myself: *The time has finally come to say goodbye to them; the people, the streets, the stars. Those rectangular slabs of concrete on which I walk now will still be slabs of concrete when I'm gone, and millions of men and women's feet will walk over them, until they become worn and they'll need to be replaced by new slabs.*

Once again the old idea which comes in moments of absolute inner calm, nagged me:

*Out there in the infinite blue cosmos, scattered and suspended in the void are billions of worlds, suns and planets, a multitude that human intellect is incapable of grasping—unable to conceive of their magnitude. And among all those mighty worlds spins a dark insignificant sphere which we call the "Earth," so be it—let it spin! Who will notice? It's like a tiny puppy running around, barking, between the legs of a herd of elephants—let it bark! . . . but on that Earth there is a continent sticking its nose out from the sea, on the continent there's a country, in the country—a city. Don't rush! . . . and in the city, a crooked street with a strip of pavement . . . patience! . . . and on the pavement, walks a creature on two legs—when you lift one leg and put down the other, that's called "walking"—they call the creature Shloyme or Shloymkele . . . what's the difference? And it suffers somewhat and thinks and it wanders around with a gun in its pocket and drinks beer and complains to another creature, with a pair of eyes, called Mirkin. And that, broadly speaking, is a "human"—it's enough to die laughing!*

—To Henia!

◆

In the company of other men, my thoughts generally find their true form; my feelings, their authentic expression, bursting with their full venom.

But I'd never felt like that in the company of women. From every touch of those soft, beautiful creatures I would shudder, something in me falling loose. The simplest thoughts and words tended to blur and become unnatural. My movements, my speech, my appearance, resembled those of a spider that had fallen into some cream. I haven't the faintest idea why that would be so. Perhaps because I was too passionate and too weak. Perhaps it was because I was young and had never been close to a woman; maybe it was because I knew neither them, nor their tastes and so never found favor in their eyes . . . whatever the reason, I suffered in their company, until the old paranoia awoke. Whenever I encountered a woman I'd grow suspicious that she would laugh at me behind my back, about my nose with the abscess to begin with, and rounding it off with the fact that I had a screw loose. I began to suspect that the entire tenderness and beauty of those creatures was designed to torment and tease lonely, ugly people like me, and, really, there was no hope of ever being able to get close to one of them. They were demons all right, no two ways about it, demons, demons, and more demons. Only *I* was made of flesh and blood. Other men were only pretending to love, to embrace late at night in dark streets, whole books are written, whole packs of songs about kissing women, about embracing women, they draw pictures of naked women's breasts, round and soft . . . to confuse me, so that I'll see what alleged pleasures there are to be had out there in the world for those with slender legs, fiery hair and eyes, and a jolly, idiotic expression on their red lips . . . All the attributes I lack . . . all to torment me . . . But I understand, for example, why when women walk past their underskirts snicker. Perhaps not all of them do; only the dresses of beautiful women laugh, while those of ugly ones merely rustle. I know everyone else hears it too, but they ignore it; it's all been arranged in advance.

Eventually my fear began to spread to all women, even the unattractive ones. I was afraid of their gaze, of their laughter, of them turning to me. I went out of my way to avoid them entirely: I didn't visit them, did not invite them to visit me, did not have any dealings with them at all. Who knows how long the situation would have lasted and how far it would have gone, if it hadn't been for Henia. I was not afraid of her. She taught me how to relate to all other women.

A radiant face, with sweet dimples in her cheeks and in her chin; kind, dark eyes, maternal eyes; small hands, warm and nervous; as soon as I'd touch those small pale hands I'd feel there was something hidden inside them, something that I too possessed. Breasts, underdeveloped for her age, almost twenty, containing an unseen nervous fire—all of this was wrapped in an austere, black dress and went by the name of Mademoiselle Henia.

When I met her she reminded me of a small autumn cloud in the night sky, with a pale, round moon shining out from behind it. Henia's mood would change several times a day. Her soul was part springtime, part autumn: here sprouting, there withering, here the sun shines, there the rain falls. In one day she was capable of speaking for hours on end, driving herself to tears, or sitting alone, downcast, and mute. She could sit there for hours, ossified, moving neither hand nor leg. Her face pale, her eyes squeezed shut as though she were straining to solve an enigma that only she knew about. And suddenly as though she'd cracked it, she would spring up from the spot, her face rosy, her eyes sparkling, filling up the room with sound and whimsy, kissing and throwing her arms around her friends as they came in to see her.

The first time I met her she didn't even look in my direction, did not see that I existed. Nevertheless, I perceived that she took an interest in me. Soon, however, she began treating me like an old friend, even tugging my hair when she was exasperated. I think I loved her a little, to the extent that someone like me can love at all. Her voice calmed my heart when everything was boiling inside. I hid my feelings, never uttering a word, never made eyes at her. Except one time, one late summer's evening as I was strolling alongside her through the park, and the damp wind picked up, I noticed that her jacket was open at her slender chest.

"You'll catch your death," I said. "Your jacket is open."

"Why don't you button it up for me then," she said without ceremony. "I'm too lazy to move my hands, they're so snug and cosy in my pockets."

I buttoned up her jacket, shivering silently.

*Such small breasts it seems, and so yielding. Warm as downy feathers and elastic as rubber.*

Henia simply thanked me and that was that.

Another time, I found her in exceptional spirits. She pulled at my hair, handed me her album, and asked me to write something in it. Such a naïve book it was, blue with two red swallows embossed on the cover. *Whoever saw the like, red swallows?* I gave it some thought and meticulously wrote:

"If I should come on foot, I'll see the face of God,
My God is ever pale and mute.
If I go out: the Devil comes to meet me—
My Devil's smile is so cold . . .
I wish to confess: 'I love you.'
But those words, too, are tired and old."

She grabbed the album from my hands and ran her eyes over those brief lines. Her lower lip quivered slightly. I noticed. But then she slapped me over the shoulder and laughed aloud. Something about that laughter disturbed me: something danced within it, something wept.

A few days later I heard that she had eloped without the approval of her bourgeois parents. Her new husband was some fellow with long hair, an accountant and a cashier at the same time. Incidentally, he's a bigshot in one of the political parties, working hard for the good of the community. If you give him an opening, he's ready to deliver a speech at the drop of a hat. I understood then the meaning of Henia's laughter. I have not seen her in almost a month, despite knowing her new address.

Now that I've dispensed with my students and banished Mirkin, only Henia stands in my way. Married now, yet she still stands in my way. She won't escape punishment though; I'll push her aside too and go *there*.

Why then have I been thinking about her this past month as if through a fog, and why do I long for her so much now?

Someone is to be pitied, but who? Perhaps it's me? Whom do I need now and who needs me? When I reached her house I was greeted by snatches of melody played on a piano. Dull, weak notes. I realized that she was sitting alone, playing to pass the time.

That reflection gave me pleasure.

◆

The newlyweds lived on the second floor.

As I climbed the half-lit staircase, I grew less and less determined. My mood sank. *What would I say to her? How will I be rid of her once and for all?* As I knocked on the door, my heart began to pound as if I'd climbed ten flights of stairs, rather than one.

"Who is it?"

"It's me."

"Ah . . . Salomon!"

I entered and saw Henia sitting by the piano, playing. She smiled without turning around. I approached and she wordlessly extended her left hand behind her back, at waist level, without looking at me, while her right hand continued to dance over the black and white keys: *Tsif—tsif—tsif* . . . as though she were driving terrified birds from their nest. Her poise made quite an impression on me, as though she'd known in advance that I was coming today and had been waiting for me, wanting to make a dramatic impression with her playing . . . *she knows I like it . . . or perhaps she is ashamed? Embarrassed that she hadn't invited me to the wedding. Ha ha, that beats all! Now of all times!*

And once again she spoke, her voice so soft and austere.

"Take a seat, Salomon, and try not to disturb me."

As I sat down next to her she gracefully snatched my hat off my head.

"In this house, we don't wear hats while seated," she said, continuing to play.

The room where we sat was a combination dining room and guest room, with a particular smell, the smell of a young couple, a honeymoon smell, seeping from the black oilcloth sofa, from the table, from the tablecloth with the blue fringes, from the lamp with the pink lampshade. From the wine-colored curtains with the embroidered floral motifs—oh those mysterious, half-drawn curtains!—which lead to the bedroom; they smile with their folds like living brows, with feigned bashfulness, unfurled . . . but they are savage beasts, they gnaw at the heart, and drink blood, that's why they are red.

And Henia sang her favorite tune in her weak but deep-chested voice, gently accompanying the piano:

"Innocent dreams, those forgotten reveries
That once we used to dream . . ."

I knew the song. Henia used to sing it of a melancholic evening, whenever a sweet, hidden fear drifted in from the other side of life. Henia used to feel the same fear as I did, hanging her head and stretching pensively.

"Blackened and heavy, storm clouds are brewing,
It's dark and damp all around.
The weeping trees, naked they sway,
Don't wake up, my lover,
Don't open your eyes!"

Now she sings the same song, and plays along . . .

"Innocent dreams, those forgotten reveries,
That once we used to dream."

The melody caressed and gnawed, tickled and stung. To quell my mixed-up nervousness, I sought an idea with which to distract myself. I noticed a picture postcard on the wall: Sakhalin Island with dreadful stormy rocks all around. *Aha, Sakhalin*, I latch onto the word, holding on like a drowning man.

*No small thing, Sakhalin: home of the notorious penal colony. When someone commits murder, be it a crime of terrible passion, be the victim the worst scoundrel in the world. How good it must be to kill such a one—but the world must do something about it, it can't just go on without him, the perpetrator needs to meet a sorry end—they'll send him to Sakhalin, to Sa—kha—lin . . . in filth and in carceration he'll linger. Drunken guards will curse him, others will distance themselves from him, he'll be driven to gambling . . . he will have to work in the swamps, in the wild taigas of Sakhalin like a horse, worse than a horse. The chains will jangle, the years will pass. And society looks on with a sanctimonious expression, rubbing its belly in satisfaction, feeling that it has achieved a fine thing, a good deed. It wages wars and kills thousands in one day and applauds . . . yet there they go, passing judgment on someone for killing a scoundrel, thereby doing a good deed . . . how can this be? I am the protest against it; with my death I will be the protest. I am free, I am master of my own life. I tunnel under the borders, breaking through—just try and stop me! Who will stop me? Who can hold me back?*

*Where is the court, the honest tribunal, the pious jury that could weigh up the merits of the death I will inflict upon myself? Whom will they sentence? Eh? One could just die laughing, I swear ... who will they send off to the penal colony? To Sakhalin———*

"Happy is he who sleeps,
who in autumn dreams of the caress of spring..."

The tremulous tones of the piano and Henia's voice grew stronger, enveloping me by force, knocking me off balance, filling me with that molasses-feeling familiar only to drunkards and sentimental thirteen-year-old girls.

*God almighty, how will it start? A start must be made...*

"You play beautifully," I blurted out awkwardly.

Henia did not hear, or pretended not to hear, her face was locked in concentration, the dimples in her cheeks hidden. Her clear, nervous hands moved, spanning the distance between the keys. Along with her hands, her whole body moved under her black blouse. Her legs moving quietly under her alpaca house-skirt. Her every limb played along. Even her shadow on the wall joined in ... and I sat, listened and daydreamed that when I'm lying cold and mute with a bloody hole in my temple, Henia will also come running, she will bend down over my dead face, will dry her tears with a clean linen handkerchief ... the handkerchief will naturally smell of clove perfume, just as Henia herself smells right now. Who knows? Maybe she will even lament bitterly. She is such a kind person after all ... And that husband of hers, the accountant with the long hair, the man of action, will quietly pull her away by the sleeve and will comfort her in the drawling voice of authority:

"Oh, silly woman, crying won't bring him back..."

And as if in a fog:

"Woe is to them that awaken in the murky, unending night;
they will never close an eye again . . ."

And the piano hums its octaves, accentuated and affirming:

"Innocent dreams, vanishing reveries—
that we once did dream!"

"Salomon!"
*Look how Henia's face loses all color right next to my face,
unsmiling.* The piano falls silent.
"Why haven't I seen you in such a long time?"
"That's how it goes."
"Why . . . yes, why did you not come to congratulate me after
my wedding? Everyone was there . . ."
I blushed—it had been a long time since last I'd blushed. *Oh,*
I thought, *how repulsive the shiney blister on my nose must appear to
her!*
But I said nothing.
"Have you ever met my Yashe?"
"No."
An uncomfortable silence.
*Yes, yes,* I thought, *my Yashe, my Yashe, what do I care? Even if
he's "yours"?*
Henia remained seated. Leaning back in her chair, she stared
at a point somewhere in front of her, and her eyes glazed over. She
drummed with two fingers on the closed piano lid.
"Do you still remember those lines you wrote in my album?"
I smiled.

Henia suddenly shifted her chair closer to mine and raised her hand. Soon, I thought, she'll pull my hair, like she used to, whenever she became elated.

But this time she did no such thing. Somehow her hand hung for a moment in the air, and suddenly, joylessly she began stroking my forehead, pushing the hair out of my face.

"Why are you so unhappy?"

*Aha*, I thought, grinding my teeth beneath my firmly shut lips, *now begins the cycle of feminine buttering up . . .*

Nonetheless I muttered:

"Just . . . it's nothing. I have a headache . . ."

And her hand continued to caress. Her hand did not believe me.

She whispered: "No, you're acting strange, you're hiding yourself . . . you're lonely."

*There you have it*, I thought to myself, noticing that she'd switched to using the familiar pronoun, *du*.

An electrified shudder flowed through my entire body, every nerve was in motion. I derived pleasure, stolen, pathetic pleasure from her gently touching my hair. My heart filled with bitterness.

*What does she want from me? What does she want? To pull me back into life? I must escape, escape and . . . It all must end.*

"Stop, Henia, please—"

My voice was weak.

"Oh, my demon, my dear demon, you suffer a great deal . . . a great deal . . . and remain silent . . . I know!" She said and fixed me with her lovingly wily eyes, "I know . . . and you keep it to yourself . . . you're bad, bad, bad . . ."

*She seems to still be talking about her wedding*—I thought—*I could have sworn she was talking about my revolver.*

And her soft hands grew ever more sure as they caressed me. I wanted to stop her but could not. I was as lowly as a slave. Everything buzzed in my brain. Bubbles swam to the surface and burst: *canceled lessons ... Mirkin kicked out ... brothel ... revolver ... I have to get started ... I have to ... I have to ...*

"What's wrong Salomon? Why have you gone so pale? My dear ..."

I suddenly realized how very, very difficult it was for me to break away for good from such a warm soul, to go off to a cold eternity. I felt that there were still many chains binding me to life, I hadn't grasped how hard it would be to break them. I began to doubt my ability to go indifferently to that filthy place, to shoot myself in the head with a sure hand, when here in this room by the pink lampshade there sits such a dear creature as Henia, capable of such forgiveness, who speaks to me so kindly, caressing my colorless hair with such tenderness. This thought frightened me, shaking me to the core:

*Any minute now I'll take out the revolver and fling it down by her feet. Right there between the two leather shoes that peek out from under her skirt ... then I'll lay down my head in that young lap ... let what happens happen ... I'll tell her everything ... through gritted teeth I'll tell her everything ...* my hand had somehow already started to reach into my pocket. But then I heard a creaking noise; the door opened behind us and in walked ...

—It was him!

I recognized him immediately thanks to his long hair. It was the accountant, the man of deeds. His face was one of those mild, "sincere," somewhat tired faces that appeal to women but men find intolerable. When you look closely, you recognize immediately a sort of unpleasant dryness in such faces, a petty egotism, cheap and cold, hidden in the lips and around the eyes.

As soon as he entered he fixed us with his gray, jealous eyes, and yet a feigned sweetness poured over his thin lips. You could tell he was raging inside: some strange young man . . . a pink shine from the lamp! A glance at his wife, a glance at me . . . and as soon as his eyes hit on my big, wrinkled nose he seemed relieved, because the sweet smile soon melted over his whole face.

Henia pulled herself toward him with her nervous, girlish body. They embraced and kissed. He had to bend down, and she had to stand on the tips of her leather shoes. My ears were practically ringing. The best girls—it cut me to the quick—end up with the worst nothings. While I, a smaller nothing, have to go and pay for sex, with pennies in the mud . . . on the day before my death . . .

"Yashe, why are you so late?"

He suddenly grew serious, very serious, puffing himself up, the foolishness started to climb, climb until it was hanging from the tip of his nose. With a coldness he slowly pushed Henia aside and sat down:

"I was very busy, mountains of work . . ."

*There seems to be a hidden meaning in his words!*

The warm feeling which had enveloped me a few minutes ago, blurred and dissipated. How, I thought, can it change so quickly? Just a moment ago his little wife and I had shared a moment of intimacy; a tenderness reserved for me and me alone . . . but a minute later she so easily gave it away to another . . . she kissed him right in front of me, leaving me to stand in the corner? What am I, a fly to her spider? Oh but I'm a spider myself . . . an even bigger spider . . . a spider one would do well to grind underfoot.

A cold hatred, a dark savagery toward myself bubbled up inside me. If I could have I would have bitten into the veins of my wrist and sucked my own blood.

—*Why had I come? Maybe to find some comfort, a stolen caress? What is that? A sweet or bitter medicine? What do I care about the young couple? What do I want from this table, from the oil-cloth sofa, from that lamp? And the revolver? Aha, the Devil dances once again around me! He wants to pull me back into life again? He hides inside a caress, in the sweet words of a young wife. He offers me cake, to stop me from crying. He will not succeed, no, no, no . . .*

My firmness and indifference were rising in me by the minute.

"Oh yes, I forgot," Henia slipped out of her husband's arms. "Pardon me, I forgot to introduce you—This is Salomon, an old acquaintance—and this is my husband, Yashe."

*Soon I will commit a terrible deed, a terrible deed*, I thought to myself brutally.

A white hand stretched out toward me, long pale fingers with a wedding ring on one of them . . .

I made a move to grasp the outstretched hand and squeeze it . . . but suddenly I pulled back . . . the terrible idea flashed in my head and I coarsely blurted:

"I don't need it . . . what do I need acquaintances for . . . what good comes from that Henia of yours and her trickery? It is base . . . just a moment ago she pressed herself against me and kissed me, the Devil knows, why lie about it? Why deceive?"

I'd hit my mark. The effect was instantaneous. They were both struck dumb as though by lightning. Two pairs of eyes turned to me and grew cold. Large, strange . . . when the shock had passed Henia began to stutter. Her lower lip hung:

"Salomon! What are you saying? You? Yashe, he says ... ? What? No, no ..."

Yashe was pale as chalk. His arms flopped to his sides like a shot goose, he bore his watery eyes into his wife's face and blathered:

"Well ... Henia ... Henenke?"

In that moment I felt like a satisfied fox that's stolen his way into a chicken coop. The fox does nothing while the hens flap and squawk, anticipating the onslaught of torn limbs. I waited. I wished with all my heart for Yashe to rise, insult me, and throw me out of the house, for him to slap me with the same white hand on which the gold ring sparkled. I would have let him. I would have stood up straight and silent ... so pitiful Henia looked. But he did nothing. He had not yet come to himself. I made to leave, with my hat in hand. My heart had stopped pounding. I was once again indifferent.

"Scoundrel!"

At least I'd managed to tease one solitary insult from Henia's lips, which had up to then been so disorientated. You could feel all her rage in that feeble cry, her offense, her entire disgust toward me from this day forth. Her cry chased after me, exploding like a bomb against my back.

I was already out the door. I could still discern the faint rustle of women's clothing. And something soft and heavy falling to the ground. Henia had fainted. And a voice, Yashe's voice, begging, wavering:

"Henia ... Henia ..."

And there you have them, "Yashe and Henia." How low they are now, how unhappy. And how fragile happiness is, God oh God. Pull one silly, hidden thread and that's the end of it.

I paused in the gateway of the building. My imagination painted a picture of the odious scene, the crude lie and venomous cynicism that I'd left in my wake, up there on the second floor, in such a new home, between man and wife, right in the middle of their honeymoon. I imagined rivers of Henia's tears and Yashe's burning suspicion, before they manage to clear things up. My conscience began to stir, slithering like a snake from its lair . . . *Perhaps I should go back? Ask for forgiveness? No, they cannot forgive such a thing . . . they will never understand. At least tell it like it was, disown the lie, the obscenity . . . What was it she screamed? Scoundrel? . . . yeah, yeah.*

But then my hands slipped into my pocket. I was fleeing, hiding from myself, to my protector, to my good, cold, metal protector. My hand sought and, like an eagle's talons, clasped it . . . the revolver . . . if I could have sunk my nails into it, I would have. A lone humorless laugh rolled out of my throat and melted into the frigid air. I walked away energetically. Squeezing the revolver in my pocket the whole way, speaking to it as if in a fever:

"No, my dear, no my love . . . we won't go back—my dear little revolver . . . never again . . . How was it Mirkin would say?—To the Devil! To the Devil! . . .

# CHAPTER 7

## THE 23RD OF TISHRE

A sleepless night, a night of wandering.

Returning from Henia's place yesterday, at a hasty, uneven pace, I began to imagine someone running after me. I looked around—there was no one. I continued—I *did* hear someone, following me with soft, cat-like steps; hugging the walls where the shadows were thickest, weaving me a gleeful, wicked trap—like a giant spider in the dark.

I began to suspect that it was Yashe, burning with jealous rage. Perhaps, having just now come to his senses, he was running after me to settle the score, for himself and for his little wife. A betrayed husband . . . sneaking up from behind, eyes bulging, frog-like, from his head; his long hair unkempt, a tangled tuft; his neck elongated like a snake. A Finnish knife hidden up his sleeve. Like a hero from *The Kreutzer Sonata.* I needed only slacken my pace for a moment for a long blade, cold and deadly, to be plunged into my back; it would have slid in through my ribs, piercing my rubbery lungs . . .

I quickened my pace.

But a moment later I reconsidered: *Well, why not? By all means, let Yashe stab me. It's all the same whether I do the deed, or another.*

And my steps became slower, more measured, I even put one hand on my lower back. I would have liked to cross both hands behind my back, as if to signal: "Come and get me, Death!" But

I needed the other hand to hold the revolver in my pocket—I had no other choice. I walked like that, waiting for something terrible to happen, for a sudden, violent attack from behind, for a roar to fill the air.

Nothing happened.

Dark figures streamed past me, meandering half in shadow and half illuminated by the shine of the gas lanterns and the moon. One out of a hundred glanced at me, without motive, and continued on their way. The others, like ants, looked only at the pavement, their nostrils emitting small spirals of vapor, which soon dispersed in the shadows.

Nevertheless, the first thing I did when I got back to my room was lock the door behind me. I remember well: the key made two turns in the lock. I put an ear against the door: no sound. Afterward I lit the lamp. Then I sat down in bed with my coat on, in my galoshes, just as I'd come in from the street. My heart and mind were empty and desolate, and yet so heavy. My head sank, as though it had been severed, hiding in the high collar of my winter coat. My hot breath, finding no other way out, burned my cheeks, my lips, my whole face.

It was only when I'd been properly warmed up that I noticed I was still wearing my coat—realizing that it was responsible for the heat, I tore it off and flung it on the floor. It makes no difference; I'm selling it first thing tomorrow morning anyway.

This was not enough to calm my nerves. I sprang up nimbly and grabbed from its hanger my new smoking jacket, which I'd had stitched a couple of months ago and which hung like a corpse on the wall under a white sheet. I crumpled it up, sheet and all, and slung it violently on top of the coat: to hell with the smoking jacket, I'm selling it tomorrow too.

I still hadn't managed to cool down, though: I kicked one leg up into the air, then the other, in so doing removing my muddy galoshes and adding them to the heap of clothes on the floor: "I'll sell it all, all of it!"

I suddenly felt unusually drained and decided to lie down on the bed to have a rest. To re-energize myself I took out the revolver, put it down on the pillow next to me, pressed my burning cheeks to it, and experienced a vague feeling of love.

"I haven't slept with you in so long, you little bastard . . . it's been ages, my dear little revolver . . ."

And a minute later . . .

"And you've been waiting so long. I've been somewhat unfaithful to you, my boy . . . you must be good and hungry, no? Admit it . . ."

My "boy" sparkled mutely.

I lay there like that for several hours without a thought in the world, sleepless and without purpose. The lamp burned on the table. Somewhere in the distance locomotives were testing their voices, bragging about who could squeal the loudest.

Suddenly I heard the heels of my shoes falling on the floor. As though mesmerized I scanned the room and understood that it was nothing. As I sat back down I said to myself, *It's simple: I could get undressed . . . really, get properly undressed . . . spread out under the covers . . . the revolver by my side . . . lovely!*

My hands set to pulling up the cover. I hadn't shaken out the mattress, or straightened it. I moved mechanically, pulling off my clothes, carelessly, as though my fingers were made of wood, losing two buttons in the process. They fell on the floor with a clink and performed a jolly pirouette before rolling away, coming to a halt with a satisfied *whirr*, and finally falling silent.

I extinguished the lamp and slid under the cover with my revolver. *Qui—et!*

Feverously, I caressed it, pressing it to my body and imagined the terrible sound that a shot would make in a silent room like this. *First there would be a flash . . . the wicked, fiery glare of an enormous demon and then: crashh! The landlord and landlady of the apartment wake up in fright, and head straight to my room. "Police!" cries the landlord, coward that he is, the landlady is so distraught that she jumps straight into the room with bare, round shoulders . . . tomorrow night that's exactly how it will be. A shame I won't be around to see it.*

The hours went by, my breath burned, locomotives whistled somewhere in the distance, and cats cried on the stairs. At first they yammered one at a time, then all together, and finally they hissed like snakes and tore with their claws . . . and sleep loomed in the air above me, so heavy, so delectable. I almost felt its taste, its odor, but it did not want to come down any lower, *it's teasing me, it's teasing.*

*Look, there's Henia. She's crying. Her tears are large and they sparkle.*

*Those are pieces of her soul that fall from her eyes. She has a soul made of diamond. The tears roll down her pale cheeks, down to her little chin. The cleft is where they want to get to. They collect there before dripping down further. Yashe's eyes are bloodshot. His long hair is straight and stiff like a horse's tail, bristly. He's holding something shining and sharp. It's tangled in a proclamation in red letters. He cries out, "Henia, my dear Henia, let me at him, let me at him!"*

*Is it a dream, or a nightmare? A nightmare by all appearances. I feel as though I haven't slept. I have proof: the whole time I felt a dull pain in my cheek. It was the revolver hurting me. I'd pressed myself too hard against it.*

*And how would it be if Henia was mine, mine alone—Not the bookkeeper's with the strange hair—and if she caressed and kissed me, really kissed me, not like earlier when I'd lied about it, but really? Perhaps I wouldn't need this bastard, when you press it to your skin it digs into you . . . Henia is softer, oh so much softer! Her hair smells like clove perfume, her eyes sparkle with a green fire in the darkness . . .*

I attempted to suppress such ragged, gnawing passions, and spit out through my teeth under the covers:

"I'll sell every last stitch of clothing, all of it!"

The darkness in the room turned blue, then pale. The gates creaked. There was a sound of sweeping in the yard, and heavy boots sniffing over the stones, which were coated in the thin frost of dawn. The pile of clothes in the middle of the room, with the muddy galoshes perched on top like a rider, slowly differentiated itself from the night, appearing like a tiny pyramid in the bluish gloom.

◆

### THE SAME DAY, 11 THAT SAME MORNING

"Step right up, step ri—ght up! Get your men's jackets, boots, galoshes, hats . . ."

*Ah, thank God.*

I leapt over to the window, tapped on the glass, and waved:

"My good man, come on in, come on in."

While he crept up the stairs, I grabbed the clothes from the floor, shook the dust off them, and threw them over the back of the chair.

I'd been waiting several hours for a peddler to show up, and had begun to lose patience. *Today of all days the peddlers decide to stay away, as if to spite me—they usually wake me up at eight in the morning*—I was ready to go out in the street looking for one.

Hush! I hear footsteps on the last steps. The footsteps of a man with large boots, down at the heel. Soon the door will creak open. My clothes as good as gone. Sleet falls on the streets outside, cold and wet.

*Selling, selling, but what about the revolver? Are you forgetting about that?*

"Good morning," I heard a toadying voice behind me. I turned around: here already. A bearded face. Red, matted hair creeping into his mouth. Watery little pinprick eyes, regarding me with the scrutiny of a shrewd businessman eager to know what sort of a sucker he's dealing with.

"Good morning. What do you have to sell?"

"Over there, on the chair . . ." I point.

The little Jew threw down his sack, scooted over to my clothes and began touching, smelling, examining them by the window—it's brighter there, he said. He skillfully rolled out the sleeves of the jacket and had a look at the lining.

"M'yes," he says, "one must also inspect the lining." And the longer he appraised the goods the more he looked at me askance, anxious.

"So . . . You're selling this?"

"Yes," I said, turning my head away.

I had the feeling that he wasn't rooting around inside a sleeve, but inside my heart; turning over my soul and prodding it with his grubby fingers . . . it felt like I was selling my last portion of life, that

I was destroying the very thing that was supposed to warm and protect me from bitter frost, and yet I smiled. Why? I don't know. It was a smile in the vein of Hugo's novel *The Laughing Man*.

"Everything, sir . . . you're selling all this?"

"All of it."

"The coat too?"

"The coat too."

He was keen to know why a respectable young man would sell such new clothes out of the blue. He inspected every corner of the room, ascertaining that I had no other coat. But he didn't want to jeopardize the deal and so held his tongue. His face took on a businesslike disdain. Coldly and cautiously he asked:

"So then, how much would you like for all this?"

"Eleven rubles" I blurted out.

*Why eleven? A moment ago the bell struck ten, so one more than that . . .*

"Come again, sir? How much?" he said, unable to believe his own ears.

"Eleven rubles, I said."

The peddler's nose drained of color. He was still incredulous, but afraid to ask again. He turned around and set to searching his pockets with trembling hands, clinking coppers.

"Well, perhaps sir would be content ha ha, with ten? Ten rubles, a round number . . ."

"Eleven!"

"Really? Sir, I cannot . . . I swear. Ten is a decent price too. What do you say?"

"No."

"I have a wife and children, sir . . . these are hard times . . ."

A wave of nausea blocked my throat. I so wanted to grab him by the collar and fling him though every door. *The very last parts of my life are for sale and he's trying to haggle, the brute! Trying to move me with his wife and children*—but my revolver, which I'd been touching the whole time in my pocket, held me back.

"My good man," I answered wearily, "Leave, please, just leave."

Just then, I felt something round and heavy slip itself into my hand. The discussion was over. A shiver ran down my spine. The man stood there, speaking rapidly, he swore, mumbling something about a wife and children. Next thing I knew he was leaving me five rubles as a deposit, swearing on the health of his wife and children that he'd be back soon with the rest. He hadn't enough money on him. He could see that I was a fine man. He'd be back very soon, mark his words, very soon . . .

I gave him a weary nod.

Once he'd left, I turned around and, with a hidden yearning, looked at my clothes—Sold.

I stood up straight as though I'd just remembered a very important matter that needed my attention. With an earnest expression I sought out a piece of chalk, took up the clothes, spread them out on the bed, knelt down on my knees next to the bed and began drawing little death's heads on the fabric, white little skulls . . . with crossed bones underneath. I've always been fond of that symbol of the inquisition, of the death court, of the future of all mankind. When I daydream I often find myself drawing such ovals, with three small dots—like a *segol*—in the middle, and stunted zigzags on the bottom. And just below that, a flat cross. There: finished! But why had I suddenly set about doing that now, out of the blue? I'd drawn a great big skull and crossbones right on my coat, along with smaller ones on my vest, shirt, and trousers . . . my knees were starting to ache. I got up and sat down on the chair near the bed. I sat there, mute, chalk in hand, eyes fixed upon the white skulls on the dark fabric. They looked like pale death-seals.

An unknown, mystical hand had stamped them onto my clothes, by the border between life and death ... the clothes were already on the other side of life ... these were stamps from the customhouse of the *other side*, it wasn't me who'd put them there, not me ...

My gaze bore into the large skull on my coat. Fragments of thoughts spun through my head: the Devil knows where those clothes will end up after I'm gone. The bugger who'll buy them will derive pleasure from them, will celebrate in them, will warm himself in their fabric ... they will be worn, someone will walk around in them in those gardens and streets where I walked in them, in the same restaurants and cafés where I sat, maybe on the very same seats, and perhaps they may even end up in distant places, in cities that I've never in my life seen, in America ... the young man who'll wear them will never know anything about it, and even if he did, what would he care? No, he must not know anything, he'll be more comfortable that way. He won't know that the one who used to wear them sold them specifically to get rid of everything he had, in order to get rid of himself and ... die. He who will wear my suit may very well hold an infatuated girl on his knee ... and caress another Henia ... that's odd, that's very odd!

Footsteps—

Swift as an arrow, I set to wiping off the skulls with my sleeve.

The fabric was dark once again.

The peddler entered, so pitiful and quiet save for his panting, like a tired horse. Drops of sweat ran from his forehead into his yellow beard. His eyes were cloudy. It seemed he'd run good and fast, afraid I would change my mind.

"Here it is, I have it all here ... one, two ... there you go, count it!"

He stuffed a pair of three-ruble notes in my hand and in one breath gathered all my clothes into his arms. So undignified. A real businessman ought to carry himself with more restraint.

I stood in the corner and watched his hairy hands trembling so avidly while they bundled up my clothes. He tied them up and they acquiesced, such quiet, soft little lambs. My coat, seemingly so big and dumb, also let itself be taken without protest, not even the least bit upset . . .

And where was I? I had to hold my tongue. I imagined a poisoned wolf in the forest. The wolf twitching in its final death throes while the black ravens and the terrible rats at once become the heros, running up, pecking and gnawing wherever they find a weak spot; wherever a sharp claw does not thrash about in convulsions . . . there's no longer anything to be afraid of. The wolf is dying. The peddler's nose is just like a snout that has been dipped in blood . . .

The clothes—packed up and stuffed into a sack. The old, wrinkled bag suddenly acquired a round, opulent belly. The peddler gave it a tender look and regained his composure. His eyes once again became bold and wily like an experienced salesman. He began wiping the sweat from his brow, looking around at the other things in my room.

"I understand, I understand," he says, "Sir is no doubt looking for a bigger place, or perhaps Sir is heading abroad? They tell me the weather's quite warm abroad . . . no?"

"Yes. I'm heading abroad."

"You see? I understood straight away"—he spotted my galoshes.

"You're probably selling your galoshes too?"

"Take them too, and go!"

The galoshes vanished on the spot.

"Perhaps Sir has a hat to sell too? Old hats . . ."

Get out of here, my good fellow!

Through the window I watched him descend the back steps carrying the full sack on his shoulders.

*Off he goes, thanking God for the bargain, for the earnings, for a good old crazy intellectual like me.*

*Oh, my good fellow.*

◆

### AFTER MIDDAY

Rain and snow, snow and rain. Oh, how shaken up I am, how everything inside me sings. A bad omen: it's raining, it's pouring, the streets are all wet. Tonight I must dash, to buy a girl with cash, and my coat is looong gone! The proof is: here's a shiny fiver, there's the rustle of a three-ruble note. No matter, I'll just dig out my old summer jacket—the one I'd stuffed under my mattress to prop it up straight. The sleeves are short and threadbare, but it doesn't matter. No galoshes either. It'll get wet, the hole in the heels will squeak, but it doesn't matter . . . nothing to be done!

Oho, nothing to be done! That reminds me of an old song: a song that haunts me like a demon, buzzing in my ears, wherever I go, I cannot sit still, cannot lie down, the words tickle the tip of my tongue:

Hear the chatter, nothing to be done,
That'll teach you manners!
In the meadows, toil the crabs,

mowing hay with hammers!

Botched and bungled, nothing to be done.

Ha ha ha, a botch!

Down in the yard below an accordion started to play. A cripple was playing and begging. Behind the wall my landlady cried out to the maid:

"Marina, where a—are yo—ou? Put on the cut—lets!"

*Aha, cutlets . . . and I haven't eaten anything since this morning. I even forgot to have some tea.* I opened up the can of sardines that I'd bought for dinner yesterday, sliced some bread and sat down to chew with all the ruckus in the background. I found it hard to stomach. My throat tightened and I had difficulty swallowing. The food was stale and unappetizing. I sat back and wrapped the sardines and bread in paper. Feverishly, I cracked open the window and flung the package out into the yard. Maybe it hit someone over the head? Never mind, they can fight back in court.

*Your Ex—cel—len—cy* he'll write, the first letter scrawled in a large swooping hand, all fancy like—fascinating, upon my word, they'll send a summons: "Where is so-and-so? he must come to court on such-and-such a day, at such-and-such o'clock in the morning" . . . "Good luck getting so-and-so to come in. Why, just a few days ago he shot himself in the head!"

Ha ha, it's a fact!

And the night is still a long way off. It's only just gone noon. I won't be able to go *there* until at least one o'clock tonight—midnight at the earliest. I still have eleven and a half hours ahead of me. Eleven and a half hours! Sixty minutes in an hour, sixty seconds in a minute. A sum of forty-one thousand four hundred seconds. One by one . . . how frightful! Sitting in this room the whole time looking out into the yard? Staring at the ceiling? Pacing from one corner to the next? That's as hard as climbing across the yard on a thin soapy wire, which is, let's say, forty-one cubits long. I'm like a fly now with the wings torn off, walking across a ball. I have to crawl and crawl, the ball is so small and yet so infinite—I can't go out for a walk without any clothes. For everyone to stare at? No, no—not until tonight.

A strange idea occurred to me though: Walking slowly from one corner to the other, a step a second, a step a second and so on, forty thousand times. Simple arithmetic, and the time will vanish without a trace!

I know perfectly well that I don't now, nor have I ever had enough patience and stamina, nevertheless I began in all seriousness. With earnest paces I measured the room from one wall to the other, stamping my heels energetically in order to confuse my agitated nerves, and counted through gritted teeth: "one, two, three . . . ten . . . thirty . . . fifty . . . a hundred . . ."

I had not even reached five hundred and my head was already spinning. The table swayed, the walls were dizzy, the numbers began to swirl and get stuck like lumps of lead pressing down in my head. My nerves put an end to my plan. *I don't understand anything, I don't want anything . . .* I reached the bed, which I had not tidied, threw myself under the covers, closed my eyes, and growled with a contrived drunken voice:

Seven little pairs of flies,
Dancing on the threshold,
Until a spider they did spy,
Enough to stop them cold.
Botched and bungled, nothing to be done,
Ha ha ha, a botch!

"Mar—in—a! Where aa—are yo—ou? The cutlets are buur—ning!"

*Aha, again with the cutlets. Here lies a young man without galoshes, without a winter coat, with a revolver in his pocket with . . . with a headache. And they want cutlets of all things! Cut—lets, again; cuut—lllets, damn them to hell the pair of them!*

◆

### A FEW HOURS LATER

Lying in bed, once again using my summer jacket as a soft pillow. Feeling everything as if through smoke. I arose again, combed my hair again. I knocked on the wall and called out for tea. Tea arrived. I sipped it. As she handed me the glass, Marina looked from me to the empty walls. She seemed to wonder where my clothes had gotten to. She noticed the white sheet missing from the wall.

"Sir is moving out?" she asked.

"No," I say, getting tongue tied, "I mean, perhaps, yes. It's hard for me to say for now—No, I'm not moving out . . . no means no! At any rate, your time would be better spent cleaning up."

"Marina!" squeaked the landlady from the kitchen, "Marina!"

My head was killing me, worse than before. I looked down into the yard through the window: the caretaker's little brown dog was running around in the middle of the yard, endeavouring, with all its might, to bite its own tail, in vain . . . and so it barked. *Dogs and their ideas!* A gray smoke poured out from a far-off factory chimney, rising slowly up to the cloudy sky and blending with the clouds, making it impossible to tell where the smoke ends and the clouds begin. And once again I shuddered, remembering how much time I had to kill before twelve tonight.

But I had to do something to pass the time. I had to. There, for example, was my old suitcase. It had been a very long time since I'd taken a look inside it.

I opened the case: shirts, socks, clothes. I'd bought most of it when I'd first started earning a little money. The rest of it was from my Aunt Zelda; she'd posted it as a gift, along with some jam and honey-*teiglach*. Typical woman! The jam had warmed and run in the parcel. To this day there are still stains of it on the shirts.

I rummaged deeper into the suitcase: there was an empty can of cocoa powder, where I keep a few trinkets as souvenirs from my childhood. One needs to keep a few mementos from such halcyon days, God forbid one should forget. I've always loved memories though, and the little things that evoke them. Here was one of my milk-teeth, my last milk-tooth, which I hadn't given away to the tooth-mouse for a coin. The tooth still seemed to chew the cookies and the kugel with raisins my stepmother used to bake when she wanted to console me for the loss of my mother, Nekhome—where is she now, I wonder, that portly kugel-maker? A few years ago my uncle wrote to tell me she'd married for a third time and was fatter than ever. "Honestly, She can barely fit in the door," he said.

Here were my colored marbles. The whole collection I'd put together as a child, paid for with the best buttons at the highest prices. All those "cat's eyes," "aggies," and "swirlies" . . . with these marbles I used to build my worlds. Blue worlds, green worlds, red and black: whatever I wanted. On a bright day it was so pleasant. All the other children played outside in the sun, but I was never with them. I would push my chair over to the open window and look through the marble into the dazzling world inside. And the world would take on the color I desired. That's how I would create worlds that belonged only to me. In my worlds there were red flowers in pink skies, a blackish sun, blue buildings, and yellow people. If I so wished, even the housecat would become green or red. My father walks past: a green father: a blue father. How ridiculous my stepmother would appear if I so wished. Ha ha, a yellow stepmother, yellow!

And here was something else—a white clod of earth from the Land of Israel. As a child, when I learned that such a piece of earth was lain by the head of every corpse, I did not rest until I'd managed to lay my hands on some, via Thieving Yankly. He was a character, that Yankly, a grandson of the *shammes* from the Burial Society. He emptied my pockets, that little swindler. I didn't know what to do with the white piece of earth, so chalk-like, but less brittle. I felt a strange sense of devotion toward it. There was a mystery to it; it spoke to me. Often I'd see the dead eyes of Yoyne Laymer looking out from it . . . The same eyes I'd seen during the purification of his body before his burial. I carried that lump of earth around with me for a good long time. I'd sit alone with it for hours, in silence. Even while studying I couldn't resist sneaking a peek at it under the table, forgetting myself . . . Now I understand that this pale piece of earth was like a childhood precursor to my revolver—a revolver that had not yet been embodied. The earth evoked such feelings in me, similar to the feelings the revolver now evokes in me. But back then they were still chaotic, without conception, without a purpose . . .

Once, at lunch, my stepmother said, to no one in particular, seemingly addressing a point somewhere between my father and the ceiling:

"What's he playing with there anyway? He has some sort of shard that he never lets out of his hand."

My father, distracted and confused as always, burned himself on a hot potato and added his two pennies' worth: "Really, is the table any place to be playing with shards? What is that thing anyway?"

"It's . . . it's earth from the Land of Israel," I whispered almost inaudibly, feeling as though I'd been spanked, or caught by a terrible misdeed. "It's not . . . I didn't . . . Thieving Yankly said . . ."

"Earth from the Holy Land!" my stepmother cried out. "And whose funeral are you preparing for?"

I remember a shudder running through my whole body as she said this.

Now here it was in my hands again. I took out the revolver and compared the two. How could it be, the revolver glows, the revolver is alive; the earth is dead . . . and yet they are close brothers . . . I looked at them and smiled.

*For the mouse!*

In a corner of my room there's a mouse hole. It's a tiny black hole, but at night the whole world passes there . . . I got down on my knees next to it, and threw in my milk-tooth. "There, now you've got what's rightfully yours." Then I rolled in the marbles, one by one. Then the white piece of earth. Having done this, I stood up to my full height and clutched my head in both hands: "Honestly, I'm not normal!"

*And if I was?*

I dismissed the idea and sat back down next to the suitcase. My tense fingers twitched.

Here was the letter from Uncle Khayim. An old letter in large, angular, handwriting. Reb Khayim is such a stickler:

> "*I've been hearing some stories about you, but what is there to say. You've frittered away what money you had and now you're starving like a dog, but there's no talking to you . . .*"

And another letter from him:

> *"Well where is your diploma then? I haven't heard anything from you. You should be a qualified pharmacist by now. You didn't want to be a furrier, no, no. You're too good for that, naturally. But what is there to say? Take a look at Alter Hoarse's son visited from Nizhny. He used to steal cucumbers from people's gardens, now he's really made something of himself, learned the furrier trade, and earns a decent living. He arrived in town dressed like a monarch, in fancy yellow boots. Fine, but with you there's no talking to . . ."*

And yet another letter from a different uncle.

> *"The important thing is to be an upstanding human being. Study and carry yourself with dignity, like a man. And if you're already a man then that's different. You can hold your head up high. Everyone makes sacrifices. You can be a pharmacist and still be respectable, you know? But if you're not a man, you're nothing . . ."*

Another letter, from an aunt this time:

> *"I'm sending you an* arbe-kanfes, *I'm sending you. Wear it in good health and write postcards . . ."*

> *Burn them!*

I crumpled up the letters, took a match and set them alight on the floor. Bright little tongues of flame, a thin, bluish plume of smoke, a gentle crackling noise.

The crumpled papers fluttered in the fire, spinning as though in spasms. They must be in terrible pain. The shine of the blaze flickered weakly on the nearby wall, the floor was already littered in black ash.

Old, moldy crumbs . . . what was that in a dark corner of the suitcase? A threadbare sack: it was my old tefillin bag. I opened it up and took out the tefillin. They were covered in a layer of green mold. It stank of damp—like the smell of a crypt. A skinny, sickly cockroach, dragging its thin little legs, crawled out onto the *shel rosh*. Tapping the four-headed "Shin" with its pale antennae, it hit against my warm fingers and fled in fear, falling in panic onto the floor. Uncle Khayim bought me these tefillin for my bar mitzvah. Two years ago, when I went to his place for Passover, I took them out, dusted them off, and smeared the straps in oil so that they'd shine.

The smoke from the burned letters had spread through the whole room. I breathed it in along with the damp and mold from the tefillin. I felt nauseous. My head began to spin. I was on the verge of fainting, so I grabbed the tefillin, threw them back into the suitcase, and stretched myself out on the bed. Red sparks still danced among the ashes of the letters. They seemed to beckon. And the straps of the tefillin hung down from the suitcase onto the floor, like the black tails of dead snakes, long, thin, and venomous . . .

Just then the maid entered without knocking. She stank of overcooked meat.

"What's the meaning of this?" I asked.

"Cleaning the room," she said.

◆

With great difficulty I've finally managed to get rid of the maid—her and her broom! As the broom so brazenly scraped against the floor, kicking dust into my face, something became clear to me, as though the sun had broken through into the mists of my brain. But the sun was too hot; my head almost burned up.

Marina had cleaned up and was about to leave. I asked her with a grateful expression:

"You cleaned up for me?"

"Yes, sir."

"No, it wasn't for *me* that you cleaned."

"Sorry, sir?"

"But thank you very much for making everything so clean."

*No, not for me exactly, but for my dead body later tonight* . . . she assumed I was making fun of her cleaning. She left, half confused, half angry. I waited the time it would take her to reach the kitchen. Then I locked the door and wrapped my head in a damp towel. I changed the towel every few minutes and poured water onto the back of my neck. It began to cool down. I tried to remember what I'd been thinking about before the maid had interrupted me.

*Stand up! I must retrace my steps and find the lost strands of thought.* A half hour already I'd been pacing around the room, thinking, and laughing to myself, quiiiietly, so no one should hear.

Well, if I am not surrounded by masked demons, as I once believed, then they must be ants; oversized bees with human faces, compelled to carry around some yoke or other, to make a racket, to have children, to lie for all their worth.—Anything to distract oneself from loneliness!—When you are alone you must come to the pure truth. The truth of all truths is death. If you are alone and die without a clear conscience—the other ants will trample you, they will crush you underfoot . . .

They despise the solitary and the disconnected: "If you are a force to be reckoned with, then we are your servants; if you are a king, we are your serfs, and you must reign over us! But what is it to remain all alone, reigning over oneself?" The world has always burned the loners, hanged them, tortured them in prisons, expulsed them, detested them, pointed a finger at them. Put simply, the message has always been: hurry up and die! Don't get tangled between our legs! We ants live, we ants walk, we walk ...

I too have arrived at the truth, the pure truth. If I had—as I'd told Mirkin—a beautiful outer shell, if I were beautiful, powerful, loving, if my blood were a little more red and a little sweeter, I would engage in the highest trickery and become a Don Juan, until ... well, until I'd used up my outer shell, until no remnant remained of it. But seeing as I don't have a shell, I'll just stick with my own truth. I would have come to it eventually at any rate.

So while I'm downtrodden, I'll do the people a great favor, and will shoot myself. Which is both the polite thing to do, and the easiest for all concerned ... I myself am the defendant, the judge, the prison, and the hangman ...

All well and good. Others like myself will come, who will get in the way of those passersby until they too are worn out ... but whether there are ten of us, hundreds, thousands, or even tens of thousands we never become entangled in the crowd ... Seeing a body such as ours approaching, people keep their distance, keep to one side, and dampen their moustaches with *eau du cologne*—others step over such bodies, cracking jokes. They fear nothing, they are accustomed to it. Before leaving the house they spray some carbolic acid on the soles of their shoes, and their trouser legs—others don't even notice us at all—always craning their necks toward the stars, seeing their futures lined up like a row of golden ducks ...

We would-be suicides, ha ha ha, we must multiply. When we number in the hundreds of thousands, millions, tens of millions, then people will become frightened. Perhaps then they will begin to reflect on the need to live differently or die differently . . . they loathe sparsity, and worship density . . . why are people so afraid of failed procreation? Why are they so afraid of barren women? Why, in respectable Europe, do we whisper so much about countries whose birth rate has dropped by a few percent, in France for instance? Why do we frown down our pious noses, such diplomatic glares, such chaste miens? Well!? There's only one rule: the more, the better, one simple reckoning; more products, more people, more people, more commotion. And the more commotion—the more babies. The more babies, the more people, so it is written . . . And there is no end to it, and nothing ever comes of it, and there is no thinking behind it . . . hush, fine! Humanity has already expanded in the hundred of millions, in the billions . . . an inundation, and for what? What's the outcome? Has it improved anything? What has it proven? Do you understand or not? Where does it all lead? Eh! My head is killing me; never mind. There's a bowl of cold water for that here, you take it and dunk your head into it up to the neck, that's it—nice and cool. I told you it would get cooler . . . You hear me, that's what I maintain anyway. Good. Many. People. So very many. Great! If they were human beings, full souls, full personalities, living artworks of nature and of the human spirit, giant butterflies—intoxicated by the summer light and by ideas, by the beauty of the world, and by their own splendor . . . it would be comprehensible. So be it, live my bipedal friends! Eat, drink, fornicate, sing, flirt, be at each other's throats . . . The Devil only knows what it's all for!—But I see Her there, there She goes, the Goddess of Life on Earth . . . I see Her: a dull face, as though kneaded from clay: unmoving eyes, turbid, bloodshot with red veins of lust and with malice . . . She stinks of intoxicating, venomous spices . . . She rides on heavy, iron wheels. Like an idol in a Brahmanist temple. From Her belly She roars: "Go forth and multiply!" And with Her teeth She grinds: Kill, strangle, enslave!—herself She gives birth non-stop, people pour out of Her loins . . .

And with Her iron wheels She dismembers those same people, Her own children . . . tearing off arms and legs, bloodying hearts, bending souls, crushing sensations, making ash out of hope and going ever forward—always the same . . . and the crushed pick themselves up with the last of their strength, driven mad by their wounds and intoxicated by Her poisonous spices, they crawl on all fours and kiss the dust where She has passed on Her iron wheels . . . oh! Exactly the same thing the half-dead Brahmanist fanatics do. After the stone idol has rolled over them . . . I very nearly did the same thing myself yesterday, at Henia's, before *he* came in, he with the long hair . . .

I see Her, there She goes, the old, bloodied whore, the earth trembles under Her heavy wheels, space roars with Her wild provocations: "Have children, have children!" and . . . ha ha ha! I'm laughing? What's there to laugh about?—I'm not laughing about that anymore: if you step, crush underfoot completely . . . no She doesn't do that. She only makes cripples and moves on—the clergy move on, Her high priests, and Her police and Her justice and pity . . . then everyone is accounted for . . . but we know, we know . . . She's the one who sends them all down. Her! They come and treat the wounded with such earnest faces, as if they could really heal with such powers, with such lively feelings . . . even enemies suddenly become good friends and help to change bandages. A cripple is no trifle! Well, are your wounds healed? Have you refused a leg for half a soul? Protected your intact limbs, and lumps of feelings with various laws? Here, have a pair of crutches as a present, and go limp over the wide, desolate earth. Kiss the dust where She has passed, love Her and She will love you back . . .

And so the world grows more full of cripples from day to day, with good-for-nothings, with unfortunates—neither living nor dead. People limp and people walk, as long as they can move. As long as there is always more . . . what for? So that the nations can boast about their statistics . . . did you hear? It's enough to drive you mad! . . . Elephants are going extinct, mammoths are already long gone, there are fewer lions with every passing year: there'll soon be hardly any trace of giraffes left . . . And the delightful broken, rotting things called humans are well protected, and they go forth and are fruitful and fishful . . . did you hear? No! Perhaps they intend to make up for their falsehood with sheer numbers? Hang on! Yes, that's it exactly; it is those who live a lie that wish to smother the truth, our truth, with their masses! We are the real truth, we would-be suicides! And they wish to demonstrate: look, see how many of us there are! Majority rules! But it won't help. They could all explode, it wouldn't help . . . the day is coming. It's coming . . . the lonely are more numerous each day, the claims are deeper, the gaze longer. The brain is growing, the legs, thinner. They sway until they come to our truth . . . Yes, I can already see corpses falling like hail . . . it's raining suicides, there's a deluge . . . they won't be able to avoid us any longer, to get away, look to the stars and ignore us, stepping over our bodies and making jokes . . . we will become a force, a terrible force . . . no more getting trodden underfoot, feet will be trodden under us . . . we will stop every current with our death current, all movements with our mountain of bodies. We will block every spring, we will hit the brakes on progress—ha ha—progress, what progress? Us! Us! Ha ha . . . you understand or don't you? Ha ha ha well, now I'm laughing. You'd be forgiven for thinking that I've gone completely mad. Ha? What's that knocking?

"Who's there?"

"Marina."

"What do you want?"

"I forgot to take the empty glass."

"Later."

"It's time for lunch."

"I'm not well."

"What were you laughing about?"

"Me? Oh, nothing, Marina. It's just that a hay fell off a *goy* wagon . . . I mean to say a *goy* fell off a hay wagon—"

# CHAPTER 8

---

It's time ... the hour I've been waiting for with such ponderous torment has finally arrived. It's time to go.

To go *there, there, there* ... to *that place* ... now I'm certain that tonight it will all come to an end. I had my doubts as I was pacing around my room with a wet towel, philosophizing. It's always easier to philosophize than to put one's philosophy into action. When you're traveling alone in an unfamiliar place sometimes you just want, with sharp longing, for the journey to keep going and going, for your destination to stay far ahead ... but the train comes to a halt: the hum of the wheels stops with a groan, the brake lets out a metallic squeak, the conductor shouts out the name of the station ... there's nothing to be done. Gather up your luggage and go!

A shiver runs down your spine.

"Pardon?" You ask again, though you heard perfectly clearly the first time, "This is where I get off?"

"This is your stop, your journey ends here."

It's already been a month now since I began gathering up all the corners into one point to bind them together in one deathly bundle. I've deliberately closed off all the paths in my life ... only one path remains, narrow and dark. So that I won't be tempted to make any detours, should my will suddenly weaken, or my determination waver, I have summoned in advance a troika of spiteful inspectors: Hunger, Solitude, and Want. They are thorough and strict. They're already on my back, beating me with glowing switches; they whip and command me: go, go further, more! Not left! Not right! Straight ahead to the house of disrepute!

Using all my willpower, I canceled my lessons, broke with Mirkin, did Henia a nasty turn, sold everything I owned, leaving me pure. We're the only ones left, the revolver and I . . . The last remaining path is also short and bare, but it leads to the red lantern. The lantern beckons from afar, waiting for me. I can already feel its red shine from here in my room. And as soon as I enter that accursed house my path will come to an end. Giant, black walls, damp and slippery, will rise up around me. One more step and I will suddenly fall deep, deep, into a cold, dark abyss . . . the bustle of life will continue beyond the walls, no living creature will be able to drag me back out . . . What is the entirety of human history to me now, or the future of the world? I am alone, after all . . .

I'm going!—now where's that summer jacket? Aha, yes, it's lying under my head. I take it out and it's all wrinkled, looks like a damp shirt after a wash. But no matter, give it a shake, straighten out the creases, and put it on. No, why draw attention to myself, take it off, sprinkle it with a little water, wrap it around a cane and leave it for a while on the table like a sheet of pasta. Yes, it's as good as straightened. That's more like it! Put it on, place the revolver in the outer pocket so that I can touch it as I walk. Ha ha, so smooth. The metal is warmed by my leg. The round tips of the bullets protrude slightly from the cylinder, like kittens.

Twelve o'clock, twelve! The clock tower is chiming now too. At night it rings out with such muffled purpose, seemingly pronouncing my sentence with the cold bloodedness of a professional, a poet, a wise man.

Half an hour ago I returned from *that place*.

As I left my room, setting off toward the red lantern, it felt as though my knees were falling out from under me. A mystical fear, expansive as the night, cut right through me, cutting—along with the cold and the rain—right to the bone. What's more, everything seemed so alien to me: my creased summer jacket, the worn-out shoes without galoshes, the weakness in my neck muscles, the carriages that rushed past, clattering in my head and splattering me with mud at the end of a long day of loneliness and silence in my room. I'd long been sick, wandering through this strange city. Everything I had—sold, pawned off, and now, barely able to stand on my feet, I went out into the streets, lonesome and pale, in search of something in a strange town, in the strange night ... but the night knows nothing, and the city doesn't want to know: it simply bustled.

The gas lanterns burned, yellow and swelling in the fog. Their gloomy shine moved lazily on the wet pavement and smiled, crooked and decrepit, without teeth. On the street corner, his back turned toward me, stood the nightwatchman, with widely spread legs, mute as a golem, while no wind blew. In the yellow lamplight his oilcloth raincoat was dripping with muddy drops.

The trees wailed and shook, naked, "*Don't wake up, my lover ... Ha? What was that? I think I'm going to need something to drink!*"

The restaurants were already closed, so I headed to the train station where the bar is open all night. There were strange smells coming from the third-class bar: the smoke of shag tobacco, and overcooked liquor, the damp peasants' sheepskin coats, and sour bran-bread in muddy sacks. And there was such a cacophony: the cursing of drunk soldiers, the nervous whistling of conductors, the heavy sighs of locomotives, the grating of packages and trunks over the cement floor, the cries of drowsy porters—the odors and the racket mixed up in my head. It seemed as if the smells were shouting and the cries stank.

I pushed my way into that miniature hell that stood before me like an illuminated island in the unending sea of night and darkness, and without glancing in anyone's direction, I made my way straight to the counter.

"Liquor . . . strong . . ."

The barman looked at me askance. He was suspicious, it seemed, of my summer jacket. Without saying a word he poured me a glass, his eyes raised toward the ceiling in a barman-like fashion. I emptied the glass in one draught and had a coughing fit like one who is not accustomed to drinking.

"Another!"

He refilled the glass. It went down like butter, my throat did not constrict nervously this time.

"A bigger glass," I said boorishly, in the way I imagined a real drinker might speak.

"A bigger glass?" The barman repeated with open skepticism, "A bigger glass costs twenty-five kopecks."

"Give it here," I ordered, with spiteful calm.

I soon lost track of how many glasses of liquor, or how many pickles with herring I consumed. But the barman was watching closely, every few moments he made a note with chalk on a small blackboard. My vision was already beginning to blur. *Who knows?* I thought, and drank, *maybe he's drawing little skulls just like me . . .*

*If you drink beer after spirits you're done for, that's the rule I've often heard from experienced drunkards.*

"A bottle of beer!"

*Look, now there's a green bottle and a glass! Just as though it has grown right out of the table.*

He poured and I drank. Pour—drink. My head filled up with hot steam. My legs—my legs were cool lead. If you pushed me down on the ground I'd have swung right back up by myself, like a roly-poly toy. Hop! And back up I come . . .

"There you are," I handed the barman a gold coin. The suspicion instantly vanished from his uneasy eyes, and by the time he handed me the change there was a smile on his face. I dropped the change into my pocket without counting it. But then I caught myself and turned around: "Have to count, have to count, you see?" He was indeed watching. He was dubious. Who needs gendarmes when you have train-station barmen?

I made a move as though I were about to take out the change, but produced a different set of coins entirely: "So, one, two . . . fifteen. Eh? That's it. *Merci, merci!*"

When I was already standing by the exit, a locomotive somewhere let out a whistle, so nostalgic and heart-rending. Perhaps it was calling to *me*. Who knows?

I halted, forgetting all about the barman.

*If I want,* I thought, blinking with drunk eyes, *If I want to travel—I can just travel, just buy a ticket and go! I have money, a lot of money! I could even go to uncle Khayim. Ho, ho, just think, Shloymke, If you want to, you could go out to a quiet place on the outskirts of the village, there are fields out there, forests. People? who needs people: You can lose yourself there . . . When summer comes—everything turns green, a sea of green . . . And you're just a black speck, a flea amid the greenery—who'd see you? A beetle flies past: zh—zh—zh—what a parade! If you watch long enough, you can see the new blades of grass sprouting in the meadow ... who needs them?* But the blade of grass grows because it needs to ... you hear that ladies and gentlemen? A five-kopeck train fair ... *The grass grows; Why ask questions? Why beat yourself up about it? It's a waste of time! Everything is green, ha ha, green, you're green too ... clouds rush by—they rush and blood rushes in your veins. It's all the same. You look, you stand there looking so long that you dry out ... you wither away to nothing! Like a drop on the sun—you are no more! Quiet, no one to worry about—green, green everything! Who asks you to like—dislike? Observe and be still. Think your own thoughts ... whatever you want ... Whom does it concern? Enough talk—take a train!*

Suddenly a second *me* interrupted, a wicked, bitter *me—A little trip? Oh yeah? That's what you feel like, is it? And what about the revolver? ...*

I stood there another while and waited: perhaps the locomotive will once again call as plaintively as it had a moment ago, you could just feel the tears in its whistle. I waited. A drunk soldier cursed somebody's mother. Out of nowhere, he called out: "Hey, you, pipsqueak!" A gendarme intervened—I resumed breathing. A miracle that he happened to pass by.

Soon I was outside again and was immediately struck by the brightness, by the dense commotion. The night and the fog enveloped me so happily, they could hardly wait for me ... *What, you want to come with me ... there? Ha ha, My old cronies! I don't think so ... look, the buildings are dancing, why don't you dance with them instead! And crack up while you're at it ... It's a celebration! A lad is going to a whore ... a celebration! It's so hard to walk, difficult, the whole train station sits on my shoulders. You can't get rid of it. Soldiers and sacks ... Oh such a wind ... a wind blows, we'll be blown away, a hero! Enjoy ourselves. Dug yourself out an old summer jacket, and to think you already had a fine winter coat ... a genuine one, with a collar, an astrakhan collar ... here comes a peddler—now!*

But the wind was so bitter, and blew with such force against the thin collar, that I had to emerge every now and then from my drunken fog and rub my frozen neck with both hands.

"You'll catch a cold," someone whispered, a quiet, worried voice—"honestly you'll catch your death."

*Aha, catch a cold*, the second "me" piped up, grinding its teeth, *God forbid, and what about the revolver?*

I walked. Carriage wheels rattled past me. *They have only one job: to spin and to rattle.* A horse almost ran me over. The coachman let out a resounding "Heeee ..." and I felt a sharp pain as he lashed me full on the back with his whip. Thinking: "Such a drunkard, an idiot." *What do you mean? Who's an idiot? Bloody hooligan ... Who's drunk? Drunk my arse!*

*I need only turn the next corner—and the red lantern will appear, soon. One more minute? Oh, I see it already ... there it is!*

I stood for a while in shock, looking up at the red lantern shrouded in thick fog. It wasn't the first time I'd seen it at night; I'd walked around here many times to scout out the entrance of the brothel, so as not to get lost when the time came. And yet I was startled. The redness of the lantern was so terrible, so angry, wallowing in the fog like ill tidings, like the reflection of a blaze on a cloudy sky in the deepest night: an isolated village slumbering as it burns to the ground ...

I was almost beginning to sober up. Retreating in shame, I suddenly became angry for no particular reason—I slammed my frozen fist into my own cheekbone.

"Take that, hobo! You couldn't have ridden in a carriage? Not worth the sixty kopecks, eh? Vagrant!"

The darkness pressed down around the establishment like a heavy sin. Frigid drops rang out hoarsely in the tin gutters—from the roof downward. *Who's dead now? The sound of coins clinking in the rusted collection box at a funeral . . . plink, plonk . . . charity saves from death*—I know I'm the one they have in mind.

—*The brothel is one of the worst,* that polite voice once again stirred in me. *It's dangerous, you can get infected by . . . the Devil only knows what . . .*

—Dangerous, is it? Infected? Hush now! And what about the revolver?

I rang the bell.

I was dazzled for a moment by the bright lights of the salon as I entered. Then features and forms began to emerge—as in a blueish steam—and I saw many strangely powdered faces, and eye-shadowed eyes looking at me like giant dolls, with decrepit, human insolence.

In passing I saw all manner of female forms, with hair in all manner of styles and colors: golden, chestnut-colored, black, double-decker, bobbed, curly, bourgeois tresses with a part down the middle, like Greek statues, artificial . . . and yet all the women there were so similar to one another—*exactly as though they were born to the same mother.* They resembled each other with their appearance, with their short, colorful skirts, with their artificial whiteness, and rosy cheeks. And it was impossible, if put on the spot, to differentiate them from their types and expressions. The same difficulty you have the first time you see a whole group of Negros, or Chinese . . .

In reality they were just women, ordinary women, and yet their faces were so alien and terrible, so new and bizarre, so mysterious . . . I felt like I'd fallen among strange beings on another planet, or even among a band of demons, disguised as women.

Both sides of the long, narrow salon were lined with soft chairs and half-sofas, upholstered in worn green and red plush. Sitting or lounging on them were the creatures with female faces, some of them fixing their thin hair in worn-out old mirrors, yawning. Opposite me, in a wide chair, sat one of them, hefty and sluggish, her legs spread wide in quite a licentious pose. There were a couple of soldiers hanging around her, patting her chubby thighs—pinching her soft flesh, while she just sat there blinking. As I entered, the soldiers paused and turned their coarse faces with salivating mouths toward me. They regarded me for a moment, laughed, barracks-style: "Ho ho ho," and returned their attention to the task at hand.

I was frightened and disconcerted by the powdered visages and the soldiers' laughter; I could feel myself sobering up. My legs suddenly became tense, ready to bolt. I searched for something to latch onto. In the corner of the room, next to the "bar" if you could call it that, stood a thin young fellow, wearing a long coat and a hat, buying cigarettes.

*Why don't I buy some cigarettes too*, I thought and approached the bar.

It's strange; my head was still so muddled and yet I felt every last thing. Everything caused me pain: the furniture, the colored dresses, the braided hair, the powder, the glances that followed me over to the bar; it all caused my eyes to sting. Apparently I cut quite the figure in my summer jacket, by the light of the gas lamps.

"What kind of cigarettes?" a hoarse voice asked me unexpectedly, and started to list the names of the brands.

"It's all the same," I answered, avoiding eye contact as I placed a three-ruble note down on the table.

A red hand passed me a packet of cigarettes, the hand of a woman, a street vendor, a butcher. The depraved creature regarded me with glazed eyes over a double chin. A compulsive eater, pure fat, without veins, without nerves . . .

"They give you a right fleecing here!" I mumbled to myself, taking back the two rubles change, "for a dozen cigarettes, what the hell!"

*And the revolver?* the second *me* added angrily.

"Looks like you're not from around here," the landlady said, her face smeared like melted butter, a sign that she was smiling.

"Hhmm? Oh, I'm just passing through. I mean . . . yes, I'm heading abroad."

"Is that so . . . abroad . . ." she said, nodding in agreement.

"*Pani, pani,*" one of the women sprawled on the couch called out flirtatiously, holding up the palm of her hand like a little girl: "Give me a cigarette!"

"Come get it yourself!" I replied coarsely, surprised at my own tone.

A flock of women formed a circle around me, asking:

"*Pani,* give me one, me too, me, Pani, me too!"

Within seconds the cigarettes had vanished, leaving behind only the empty box in my hand. I bought a second packet, and that too was soon emptied. Pale fingers with fashionably pointy nails, grabbed them from the packet, while powdered faces, faded and tired, smiled at me without shame or warmth, revealing badly replaced teeth.

As soon as I'd treated the girls to cigarettes I became a candidate to sit on one of the soft chairs.

*You may. You may sit*, I assured myself, *even in a summer jacket.* I sat down.

I pulled on my lit cigarette with all my force, with affected appetite, seemingly jumping on it like an inveterate smoker after *havdole*, biting the filter, hoping to compose myself. A feeling of nausea spread in my throat, on my tongue. The smoke poured like poison over my ravaged gums, my palate burnt by liquor. Nevertheless I smoked ever more zealously, thirstily sucking in my cheeks, almost forgetting why I'd even come here in the first place, surreptitiously stealing glances at the strange creatures who were lying around and laughing half-heartedly, smoking my cigarettes.

*Honestly, here I am sitting in a bordello; imagine what Uncle Khayim would say if he could see me now:"Where is your diploma now? Well this really takes the biscuit."*

It turns out that the night was only beginning for them. There were no clients apart from me, the young fellow in the long coat, and a couple of soldiers. I watched as Long-Coat grabbed one of the girls by the fleshy part of her arm and pulled.

"Want to hop into the saddle?" she asked, as nonchalantly as if she were suggesting a simple glass of tea.

He nodded yes, gave her a flick on the nose, and dragged her off.

This performance discouraged me; my heart clammed up, and I felt I was going to throw up everything I'd eaten that day.

*You can still run away . . .*

"Yes, ha! Run away! What a blackguard! Today's the day you'll take one of them, this very night you're going to —"

*A death! For shame!*

I sprang up suddenly, like a bouncing rubber ball, and did something I hadn't planned on doing.

"Leave her, leave her," I exclaimed, arrogantly barging past the soldiers who could not keep away from the fat one.

They stepped aside without protest.

"Come on," I said to the fat one, who was leaning back in her chair. I nervously fidgeted with a button on my jacket.

She looked at me with blank, surprised eyes, the bovine eyes of a cud-chewer.

"Come on!" I said more forcefully, grabbing one of her limp, warm hands. But as I did so, a shudder ran through my body from head to toe and I released her sweaty hand, such was the repugnance I felt.

For a split-second I'd imagined she was my stepmother . . .

"Well, go on then!" the landlady encouraged her from the other side of the counter.

The fat woman let out a disatisfied sigh, shifted her weight, and prepared to lift herself up like a pregnant woman. The color drained from my face and I flailed my hands in protest.

"No, no, not her—I'm—not her—"

I moved aside.

"Ho ho ho," the soldiers laughed once again, without a jot of respect, and returned to resume their interrupted amusement.

"Come on then, make your choice," the landlady advised me, like one who only wanted what's best for me, "What are you waiting for? Spoiled for choice, eh?"

But I'd already slipped my hand into my pocket and gave my revolver a squeeze. I stood, resolute and indignant.

"I know, I know," I growled bitterly and looked frantically from one powdered creature to the next.

In a corner I spotted a short, pale girl—skimpy red underskirt, pert little nose, blue patches under her eyes—sitting by herself, separate and silent. I beckoned to her with a finger. She came right over and smiled. But her greenish eyes remained cold.

I followed her up the steel staircase that lead to her room on the third floor. She led the way, leisurely, like someone with time on her hands. I dragged myself after her, hypnotized, and noticed what a fragile neck she had, such slender, shapely legs, and taut black stockings. Such a pale girl with a neck like that had no business standing there on the steps, turning to me and saying in a drowsy voice:

"You know it costs a ruble, not a penny less."

"What?" I said, offended, "... well I might just give you *three* rubles."

"Hand it over then."

And she skeptically extended a slim hand with blue veins at the wrist, her fingers folded in the shape of a paper boat.

I handed over the money.

And once again—the short red underskirt, the taut stockings. I climb, my half-closed eyes, stinging as if in a thick smoke. I touched the revolver in my pocket and fragments of thoughts bounced about inside my empty head:

*Fat ones everywhere: a fat stepmother, a fat landlady ... for once, at least, a skinny one, a skinny one for once.*

◆

Once I was all alone with her, I again felt discouraged, and started furtively scratching the abcess on my nose. Here, sitting next to me on a stool was a woman, an actual woman, a real woman with loose hair and a short, short red underskirt ... But I asked myself: *How could it be? Why was she not nervous? Why was she so dispassionate?*

*Here we were sitting like husband and wife after all—all alone! Why do her eyes not sparkle?* It seems it's all a ruse, feminine wiles, to inflame my lust all the more.

Or . . . wait! Perhaps she's not a woman at all—and this room is not a room, it's all a pretence, a hoax! Her powdered face, her pert nose are not . . . are somehow not what they seem.

I touched the nape of her thin neck with my fingertips, to ascertain if she was made of flesh.

"Oh! What cold fingers!" she cried out, nervously crinkling up her face. She seemed so much older . . .

I blushed and turned away.

"My dearest," she said, suddenly caressing me, grabbing me by the shoulders. I looked her straight in the face, but her eyes were just as cold and distant as before.

*Such a small slip of a thing and yet she knows the profession so well.*

"What?" I said, also turning frosty.

"Why don't you treat me to a little something to drink?"

"Is there brandy here?"

"In a manner of speaking."

"Here you are," I said, handing her all the money I had in my pocket. "Get us some brandy, damn them all!"

Suddenly letting loose, I peeled off my damp summer jacket. Recklessly, as it happened—the revolver made an audible *clank* as I placed the jacket on the chair.

"What have you got in there?" She asked, stopping and craning her neck.

I went pale. *That's all I need . . .*

"Nothing. You have to know everything, do you? You'd best worry about the brandy instead. Hurry up! Get the best stuff, the strong Finnish stuff."

And I gave her nose a flick. Just like the man in the long coat earlier . . . but with more panache. She left and I heard the patter of her yellow shoes as she went down the stairs. I rushed over to my jacket, folded it neatly so as to better hide the revolver, and put it away in the corner. I tried to relax.

The room was lit by a paltry lamp in a tin can, the walls were covered in pictures: the suspicious and debauched faces of naked men and women looked down at me, laughing. I was especially disturbed by the dirty mug of one particular fellow: with a shaved head, showing off his large horse-like teeth, beaming, beaming constantly with a depraved grin . . .

*Someone's coming! It's her with a bottle of brandy and some glasses.*

"Oh," she said, "it's hard to open."

The long cork made a kiss-like smacking sound as it parted ways with the bottle . . . suddenly there were two flutes full of a brown liquid, their long necks shining.

Such a slip of a girl, with such a little button of a nose and yet she knocked it back like an expert, a seasoned drinker, bringing the glass to her lips, skillfully throwing back her head, until it almost touched the headrest of her chair, and pouring the sharp liquor straight down the hatch, as though down a drain. At the same time she'd put her other hand under her chin to catch any fallen drops. Then she brought the empty glass down onto the table with a bang, and let out a feverish: "aaahh," a shiver went through her two shoulders, she made a sort of growling noise and refilled her glass. What can I say, a consummate professional! And so I drank, fumbled, laughed, and grimaced, the brandy spilled on my knee, and on the table. I drank until my head felt like a plume of steam . . . My heart was no longer a tight ball of pain and shame. I stole a drunken glance at her: that slender profile and her bare neck started to appeal to me. A sentimental tenderness built up inside me, a gloomy drunken compassion.

"Do you like this life?" I asked, tentatively putting my hands on her shoulders, her delicate shoulders.

"Do I like it? Why not," she laughed. "Every day a new man. What's not to like?"

"And the landlady lets you go to the theater? There's such a thing as theater, you know."

I pressed myself against her.

"Theater? What would I want with theater? There's a piano here too, and Zoshka can play on it like nothing else, better than any theater!"

With silent, burning lips, I pressed myself against her unbuttoned bosom. Such drooping little breasts she had, so small and naïve you could almost weep.

"A lot of people have touched you like this, a lot of rogues, eh? It's intolerable . . . was it a lot?"

"Listen, give me another two rubles," she said hoarsely. She laughed so close I could taste the liquor on her breath. So skinny, so small.

"Just like Yashke and Henia, like Yashke and Henia," I babbled, kissing her ever harder and longer, "just like a couple of young newlyweds, you understand? "

"Who are Yashke and Henia? Come on, hand over another two rubles, you're an educated man, I can tell. You're good for it. Where's your coat? you've got loads in there, I heard it clink just before."

"We're both so wretched," I babbled with overwrought compassion, almost with tears in my eyes, "we're both wretched, are we not?"

"Come on. You've got more money in your pocket, a cultivated man like yourself . . . show me, empty your pockets . . . the coat too . . . there's silver rubles in there, a whole packet, I heard it. Come one, just a ruble . . ."

"You sell your body in order to feed yourself . . . wretched, while I . . . never mind, it's all the same."

And somewhere in the back of my mind: *not that, don't talk to her about that.*

"Will you buy me a golden ring with a ruby, like Zoshka has? A red ruby! Go on, you will, an educated man like you . . ."

"I'm telling you, you don't get it, both of us—like Yashke and Henia. He has a golden ring. He gave me his hand . . . I —I don't . . . Embrace me, finish off the bottle. Hold me tighter, Uncle Khayim will never hear about it, never."

Instead of an answer two drunken hands crawled into my pockets and groped around.

She reeked of brandy and cheap cologne. The flame in the lamp began to rise, to smoke.

— — — — — — — — —

"Was that your first time?"

"What? I don't . . . yes."

I put on my jacket with the agitated movements of a man trying to pull himself out of a cesspit. I could still feel the touch of her naked body on my skin.

Those parts of my body that had touched hers burned as though smeared with mustard. The room was full of soot. The lamp flickered.

"Like a wavering soul," I thought. Wet snow was beating against the windowpanes.

"Leaving already?"

"What? That's enough. No more."

As I reached the bottom step, she ran down, half-naked, and squeezed past me into the salon where she whispered something to her friends.

I was greeted by sniggering and whispers: "His first time, his first time." A glowing shame and a terrible disgust lifted me up like a wave and pushed me toward the door. I felt the cold, brass doorknob in my hand. Behind me the laughter and whispering continued.

Unexpectedly my left hand slipped into the pocket of my summer jacket . . . the revolver!

I relaxed at once, turned around and glared at them sternly with a furrowed brow and a cool smile on my lips.

They promptly fell silent.

"Beggar, what's troubling you?" One of them said, offended.

"Nothing," I said, calmly lifting my head.

I went out.

◆

### AFTER A GOOD WHILE LYING IN OBLIVION

The lamp is still burning on the table. My impressions of these last, accursed twenty-four hours are so numerous and vivid, so stinging and confused. It feels like my overstimulated brain is wrapped in iron barbs. If it wasn't for the revolver, my dear sweet revolver, refreshing and invigorating me with its smoothness, with its nickel smile, I'd have lost my mind. I'd have torn off my clothes and run around in the streets, screaming in torment. My memory sways inside me now, slow and tired like a light that's about to go out. Now my memory rises, flashes, I imagine, I remember ... and now the flames of memory subside again. I throw myself into bed, stretch out my limbs and lie there as though unconscious. Everything is dark and squalid, fermenting lightly like dough left out for too long. Without form, or energy.

When I left the salon and came out into the courtyard it was colder than before. Snow pelted my face with lithe, icy whips. But I no longer felt the chill; my skin was burning ... And by the time I made it across the courtyard and reached the gate, I was so worn out that I saw green before my eyes. There was a flat piece of iron protruding from the snow in the shadows by the door, I fell onto it with my burning temple and felt nothing. I became nothing more than part of the darkness. And the damp snow fell and fell in the shadows; it seemed to weave a web, above me and around me, of sticky gray threads, trying to tie me to the gate for all eternity. My head was empty and glowed hot like a pot in which all the water has been boiled off. I stared with dull stubbornness at the red lantern which was swaying high on a pole a few paces from the door, its dreary, red shine like a large sinful stain crawling back and forth across the muddy snow.

Just then I heard footsteps approaching. I quickly straightened myself up and listened. A flicker passed through the fantastic red shine of the lantern: a student's hat and another head. One step closer and the second head came into focus—

It was Mirkin!

I was stricken by a horrifying dread, which filled my entire being. It was the kind of terror that can turn your hair gray in a second, the fear of a nervous fanatic who sees a shroud-clad corpse appearing in the darkness. The fear knocked me backward like an iron hand, pushing me behind the door of the gate, which was still open into the courtyard, compelling me to hold my breath, and wait. My heart beat fast and heavy. Each time it seemed on the verge of stopping, it would pound again abruptly, resounding in my ears. I had no idea why I was so frightened, why I had hidden myself away like a thief. The sliding of galoshes over the damp cobblestones, the pecking of walking canes—

"The blonde one? Her, the Polish girl? Oh she's a dab hand alright..."

Mirkin's voice.

"Shhh. Listen! Over there, someone just moved and hid themselves... wait! Who is that?"

"You're imagining things."

They stopped in their tracks. The walking canes fell silent.

"No, really, there's someone there ... I hate these sorts of pranks. Who's hiding there? Show yourself!"

And the iron tip of a cane crashed obstinately against the door, right beside my ear.

I felt cornered like a trapped animal; they weren't going to back off. I had only one second to figure out how to escape this shameful predicament.

"Who's asking you!" I suddenly screamed, jumping out from behind the door.

They both took several steps backward in fright. The red light of the lantern fell on the three of us. Three pairs of eyes met each other's gaze.

"Sa—a—lamon?" Mirkin sang out in astonishment, his eyes bulging like a carp.

"Who's asking you?" I said through gritted teeth and lunged straight at them.

They jumped out of my path, dumbstruck.

As I walked away, I turned around and cried out again.

"Who do I listen to, eh? I wanted to go in ... in—to the whores, and so I went ..."

"Is that Sal—a—lomon?" Mirkin asked again behind me, drawing out my name.

I had an intense desire to mimic his sing-sing question with loud derision, twisting my whole face so that my mouth should appear on my right cheek. But I held back with all my restraint and strode off, at full pelt, into the night. The falling snow came between us like a dark gray wall. I was alone once again.

I bit my lip in embarrassment. I understood that I'd acted like an imbecile. I could have walked through the gate with my head held high, proud, instead of hiding like a mouse, not saying a word. The thought exasperated me even more.

"Who asked them?" I balled up my fists, *such swine, what business is it of theirs? I wanted to go, so I went, and ... I don't have to ask anyone!*

◆

A few lone carriages still passed through the streets. Lonely people, with or without umbrellas, they ran quickly past me on the pavements, hiding their faces behind high collars, hands in sleeves: heading home, home, home! They resembled giant bats with torn wings, fluttering every which way, attracted by the light, by the warmth, to the safety of their own four walls. *But what do I have to hurry for? D'you see? It's snowing, let it. What's waiting for me? I still have time.*

My footsteps slowed, became hesitant. All of a sudden I felt something akin to animosity toward my revolver, which was swinging in my pocket, hitting rhythmically against my side, reminding me not to forget . . .

Whenever I passed a streetlamp and encountered some woman, I quickly stepped aside. Their smooth faces, the rustle of their clothes, called up an unnatural disgust within me. I've only experienced such aversion once, when I lay in bed suffering from a bout of typhus and saw a fatty lump of roasted meat on the table. I attempted to remedy my nausea: for every woman that passed I spat out. Walking and spitting, walking and spitting. Spitting into the damp snow.

◆

Similarly, when I was already close to home, I unexpectedly found a pile of copper and silver coins in my jacket pocket. Miraculous! I'd figured the *little one* had given my pockets a thorough search.

*What good is it to me?*

I gathered the coins together in my hand and let them slip through my fingers, flinging and sowing as I went along, a step—a coin, another step, another coin. Those round, flat pieces of metal with their embossed lettering, which had up to now played a bitter role, now represented only humiliation. I have yet to die, they are already dead, their tiny trapped souls have already flown off. In my hand all that's left are hard, superfluous bodies. *Madmen*, I smiled to myself morbidly, *and with these things you can acquire anything, anything . . . even "love," even naked twelve-year-old children who still smell of their mother's milk. I myself have only just now paid for "love," even someone like me ... madmen! One person deceives another and another, until eventually everyone is sold ... madmen!*

It was all so pathetic, so bitterly sweet to fling away those lifeless metallic wheels—so innocent, so sinful—in the middle of the night, over the muddy and snowy ground. Where the snow was thick, the coins vanished without a sound, as though into cotton. And where the snow had melted somewhat, I'd heard a slight tinkle—*"plick"*—staccato and toneless.

I spotted a beggar on the corner, standing hunched over his cane, groaning.

*You see that? Even in the middle of the night you can't get away from them ... here I am and he couldn't care less. Such a beggar! He wants a donation so he does ...*

Nevertheless I approached him and, with a silent gesture, I handed him the remainder of the coins.

His long body, wrapped in rags, bent over double.

*Is he bowing for the Devil, or what?*

And in a hoarse, exhausted voice he said:

"Oh *Pani, pani*, may God grant you happiness, success, and a long life."

"Happiness? Succ—ess? I whispered and stared at the beggar right in his dirty face. "Ah! A long life ..."

I don't remember clearly, but I have the impression that the words "long life" provoked a fit of wild laughter. One thing I do remember, though, is that suddenly the beggar grew frightened and ran off, with one lame leg and with a crutch: *clop—thud, clop—thud ...*

◆

Once again I find myself on my bed, immobile, without a sense of self, staring at the ceiling illuminated by the shine of the streetlamps. I had the sensation that I was lying in a bright, yellow dough: the whole room was filling up to the ceiling with a viscous, sticky substance, while I lay there unable to move ... the substance slid into my mouth and I got the taste of overcooked liqueur and rotten herring.

Something moved in the room, slowly, quietly, like a cautious burglar. The movements grew ever faster and more frequent. The walls began to dance. The runny dough started quivering in yellow waves ... I swayed along with the waves as I lay in bed, up and down. I was afraid to stretch out my hand, or shake a foot, as though I were lying on a narrow plank in a seething river.

I did not understand at first, but my mind tremored, fluttering with buried panic. I felt the urge to scream, but could not.

The fear enveloped me, tighter and tighter. I strained to focus all my diffuse, fragmented feelings into one spot. Until I finally understood that it was nothing; there was no reason to fear. It was only the oil in the lamp that was running out, and the flame flickering, in death throes, waging war on the darkness.

*Splutter—crackle* ...

The flame in the lamp and the large fragmented patches of jaundiced light writhed in agony, twitching on the walls in fantastic convulsions. All the while the shadows lunged at them, beating them with black bat-wings.

*Crackle—splutter* ... It sounded like the inside of a chicken coop and then: chaos, nothing ...

I opened my eyes again and the room was completely dark, save for a faint satin-black sheen from the windowpanes. Melting snow was running down the outside of the glass. A loose sheet of metal on a rooftop was banging with great force.

I felt heavy, my feet were frozen to the bone, my whole body drenched in sweat, my head was rusted lead.

*The revolver* ... the first thought crawled in like a filthy worm, *perhaps it's time.*

I listened, imagining I could hear something. Yes. Murmuring in the dark. Regular and still ...

It was the gentle ticking of the steel heart of my pocket-watch, which I had left on the table.

I hadn't noticed the ticking earlier ... but now that the lamp had gone out my eyes were left with nothing to occupy themselves, and my ears began to pick up an industrious, steady clicking in the darkness:

*tik, tak, tik, tak, tik, tak* ...

I lay still for a few moments and listened, hypnotized, to the ticking. Animosity bubbled up gradually inside me, until it became clear that I would need to come to an arrangement with the clock.

*Would you look at that, such industry, such haste! It has no intention of stopping, why's it ticking like that, the damned thing! Who's asking him? "Tik tak—tak"* ... *Aha, I understand, it can't wait* ... *it's counting down my final seconds* ... *every second it slices off another piece of the one and only thread that I have left, announcing: soon, soon* ... *it's an enemy, a hidden enemy* ... *it's laughing at me: "tik tak tik tak": it's all the same to me tik tak. It's not you, I'm ticking for someone else, tik tak* ... *Well, I'll show you, just you wait, you wretch!*

Quickly and with all my remaining energy, I got out of bed. The mattress squeaked behind me, startling me. For a moment I stood there, erect and mute like a shadow. Then I cautiously made my way, in the darkness, from the bed to the table ... *tik tak* the watch ticked at me, playfully and merrily, as if to say "What do I care ..." Like a cat I shifted my weight, one step after another, until I scraped my belly against the sharp corner of the table and stopped. I groped around on the table until I found the watch and let out a moan of pleasure. The chain hung from my hand. "I have no beef with you," I said reassuringly, detaching the chain and placing it back down on the table. Only the watch now remained in my hand, *such a measly thing!* Even sitting there captive in my hand, it did not stop counting my final minutes and laughing at me: *tik tak tik tak ...*

I stood for a moment with clenched teeth, closed my eyes with ecstatic malice, then bent down, cautiously, laying my captive on the floor. I placed my right heel firmly on top of it, held on to the table and raised my left foot in the air, so that my entire body weight was concentrated on one spot.

*Crack ...* I heard a sharp snap of trodden glass and crushed steel cogs in the dark, I shuddered from the suddenness of it all and stood there on one foot, biting my bottom lip. I was afraid in case the noise had woken someone up.

Everything slept as before. Only the loose sheet of lead outside the window continued its clap, clapping ...

Then I knelt down on one knee, put my ear to the shattered watch, and listened.

Silence.

It had stopped ticking.

"Aha, what's this now?" I muttered, saturated with vengeance, "you're finished? You're not laughing anymore, finished counting, finished reminding, eh?

But I soon stood up and trained my eyes on the darkness:

*But you must die anyway, madman! What! Nothing accomplished . . .*

I paced around the room for a few minutes, trembling, rubbing my cold hands. It seemed as though the broken watch's little soul was still hovering about in the air, laughing, *nothing accomplished, nothing. You must die . . .*

I crept around in the dark and heard a ringing under my feet.

I'm a dead man, but *this* still lives?

Then I groped around until I found a tattered notebook, bend down and started sweeping up the pieces of glass and the broken cogs . . . *so as not to step on them* I thought smiling satisfied. Having finished I put the notebook back down; *Now what?*

I drew nearer the window and saw that a thick fog now hung over the city. You couldn't even discern the outline of the rooftops or chimneys, just pale circles of light flickering from that part of the night. They were so similar to the artificial eyes of *those* ladies, in *that place . . .*

*May you choke, each and every one of you, once and for all!* I cursed the sleeping city in my heart.

I moved away from the window, agitated, and thought:

*They're laughing too. They'll still be burning tomorrow and the day after tomorrow too, a year from now . . .*

All of a sudden I had a desire to examine my appearance, to see what I looked like now. The mirror hung somewhere in the darkness, forgotten and blind like me. Next to the unlit lamp I found a packet of matches, there were only a couple of dry matches shaking around inside.

*Sssss*—one match lit up with a venomous hiss biting my eyes . . .

By its tiny fluttering light, uneven and yellow, scraggly sweaty hair appeared in the mirror; sunken pale cheeks, savage eyes—they were somehow larger than usual—riddled with thin, bloody little veins, and blinking in pain.

I looked at the unfamiliar face and my heart beat heavily and unevenly. It was horrifying to see such a brow, a nose, lips, horrible to see such hair on that head! And those shoulders too, those shoulders too . . .

When the match went out and I found myself once again in darkness, the old notion came to me: *Ha, maybe it's not my face at all, not mine . . . I'm wearing a mask like everyone else; I only think that I'm a person.*

Lighting the second match, my face again appeared in the mirror. This time I stuck out my tongue, long and insolent. The face in the mirror did the same. I quickly pulled a hideous, twisted grimace. the crooked, distended smile of an idiot. The face in the mirror became just like mine. No sooner had I seen it then my eyes winked craftily—the same thing appeared in the mirror. And I don't know why, but the whole time, fragments of thought floated through my mind without any context:

*Mirkin. Red lantern. Yashe, revolver, Uncle Khayim.*

"That's my face, my face, mine?" I mumbled, and when the second match went out, I lit the third and final match.

"I told you," I said shaking my fist at my reflection, "I told you, you blackguard, that . . . that eventually you'll die a horrible death, I bloody told you!"

The man in the mirror also shook his fist. I felt my finger burning and let go of the match. The flame gazed up at me from the floor for a second with a choking red eye, shrinking. Shrinking. A speck. Gone. Dark.

The empty matchbox fell from my hand.

Like an offended child, who'd been promised a treat but didn't get it, I stood in the dark, alone, beside the blind mirror. *I shouldn't have used up all the matches so hastily, devouring what little light there was with those three thin splinters. The light has all been eaten up and now I must stand in the dark!*

I felt restless. I wanted to protest against the darkness in the room. If I hadn't been afraid of making too much noise, I know what I would've done. I would have broken the mirror, with my fist—it had to be with my fist. May the glass pierce me until I bleed! One punch *crashhh* . . .

And no more mirror!

◆

## DAWN

I don't know if I slept, or if I merely passed through a feverous state of forgetfulness, but when I started to become aware of my surroundings I saw that I was lying in bed, still fully dressed, my legs like lumps of wood. I don't remember when or how I'd ended up in bed.

I felt a tickling pain in my throat. I tried to make a noise, attempting to scratch the itch by forming guttural consonants. A muffled croak was all I could manage, a hoarse, tattered nothing, an inhuman voice. It seems I'd come down with quite a cold last night, in my light summer jacket, my throat had completely swelled up.

A late autumn dawn, a pale shine peeping in through the windowpanes, tired, and unsatisfied, whitening the darkness, melting into it like a drop of milk in a black liquid. When you wake up in such a gray shine with a swollen throat, with frozen, wooden feet and a groggy head, a desperate weariness dominates your every limb, a desolate disgust toward everything.

Bury your head once again under the pillow and let it be day, night, dusk, whatever it wants . . .

But an unseen hand grabbed me: a voice without a voice commanded sternly: *Stand up!*

I stood up.

I shook myself and bit my lip, thinking that the pain would warm me. I don't know if the cold was an external one for want of heating, or if it was coming from inside my own body. In either case the chill was penetrating. I'd never in my life endured such bitter cold, as though my skin had been flayed off, exposing my muscles to the freezing air like those people in Henia's medical books.

I have two shoulders. Yes. Two arms hang down loosely from them. Unfamiliar. I lifted a hand and gave my forehead a rub. Strange—that's no head. It's—the Devil alone knows, but it's not a head.

I once again tried to force a noise through my swollen throat.

I stood like that a while in the middle of the room. My knees burned, frozen ants crawled over my back, but my heart was empty and at rest. I only felt that, if I wanted, I could root around in my memory and I'd surely remember *something* . . .

But deliberately, almost artfully, I endeavoured to avoid remembering *that thing* . . .

"Well then, my good man, what now?" I said aloud, wincing slyly to myself.

*Nothing, my good man, nothing . . .*

Seeing the table, I address it in a simple-minded whisper: *There's a table, and there's the chair one sits on. You sit on it. Those are the walls of your room. Walls, ten rubles a month you pay for this room.*

"Ten."

*Well, if that's the case then sit yourself down on the chair . . .*

I frowned and smiled submissively, like one who is afraid when an elder gives an order, and sat down.

*If I'm not mistaken your name is Shloyme, or Salomon—or back in your father's house—Shloymke.*

"Shloyme, Shloymke," I croaked through my swollen throat.

*Hmm, I was under the impression that you wanted to . . . as it were . . .*

"What?" I startled myself. "I don't understand. Why do we need to do away with ourselves?"

*Listen, do you want to shoot yourself or don't you?*

"Yes, yes."

*You remember? With the revolver!*

"With the revolver."

*You're not having any regrets, Shloymke . . . as they call you there, are you?*

"No, no, no."

*Well then in that case why are you trembling?*

"It's cold? Autumn. No clothes? No lessons. Henia . . ."

*Oh, imbecile, spit on them all, spit.*

"Tfu!"

*That's it.*

Pause.

*Tell me though, what are you waiting for? Where is . . . What's it called? Where's the revolver, the revolver!*

"Here in my pocket."

*Take it out, take it out!*

"Soon."

*Take it out right now! Show it!*

"Here."

*That's good. That's good.*

Pause.

That was the evil "me" inciting, proud and bitter, cursing, urging my frightened and weakened self a whole night long toward the revolver—it saw the weapon and it suddenly turned tender toward me, so devoted, so palely joking, like a wicked father to a child who will soon undergo an operation.

*Are you afraid?* He said to me, once again smiling tenderly.

"No."

*Well then, stand up. That's it, go over to the window. That's it. You see how it's raining? You see those clouds? The earth is damp, and ugly . . .*

"Ugly, ugly . . ."

*You see those rusted iron roofs? They're wet? Smiling decrepitly, are you sorry to see them go?*

"No. No."

*Windows gleaming black. Pallid walls. Unhappy people suffocating out there, cold.*

"Unhappy. Cold."

*Shleymke! Where has all our hatred gone? Our nerves and envy? The past and the future have become entangled. The borders between good and evil have vanished. What is holy and what is unclean?*

*What is truth, and what are lies? There's no beginning, there's no end, nothing . . .*

"Nothing."

*No, not nothing. There's still an abscess left over, an infected sore, as large as the globe . . . it feels only its own pain, with eternity. Eternity is us, us and us alone, a great pity for them that are still alive . . . what was it the Crucified One said?*

"Him? 'God, forgive them, they know not what they do.'"

*No, that wasn't it, "God, forgive them, they know not what they live," that's how it went.*

"Yes, that's it."

Pause.

And suddenly:

*Listen, you're slipping away again. I don't like it. It's almost day. Get up! The barrel of the gun to your temple. That's it. Now, count: a one, and a two, and a three. Finger on the trigger. Count!*

"One, two . . ."

And there my finger lingered. A foggy curtain was suddenly lifted. A horizon revealed itself. My mind lit up, every corner of the earth became bright, bright. My two "me"s fused together. I felt that right now, this very moment, this wide earth is full of many like me, lonely, broken people. One foot here, the other foot already on the other side of life . . . Everything is transparent! I see them all around, all around: in Paris and in London and in New York and in Fez and in Bombay, in towns and villages . . . Perhaps in the same city as me . . . They're standing right now in every corner of the earth, young and old, with their murder-weapons in their hands. The same feeling in their hearts, the same grief in their eyes . . . the same as me. In the same moment that I shoot myself, in every corner of the world dozens will also shoot . . . Ho! One triumphant shot into eternity, one thought ... thousands and tens of thousands of miles away from me, they will fall down dead along with me. Many like me, many ... On grass, on a straw mattress, in attics, on plush carpets and on silk cushions ... Girls with pale breasts, whom no one has ever touched ... I feel their breath, I see them. I'm not alone, I'm not alone:

A warm love, mystical and new, as large as the cosmos pours through my every nerve. My lips mumble as in ecstasy:

"Greeting to you all, gr—eeee—tings ... "

And at once the fog returns, the world is gray, the horizon—narrow. My hand trembles next to my temple ... *That's something I had not anticipated—*

"Three! ... "

—  —  —  —  —  —  —  —  —

*August 1905*

# GLOSSARY

**ANGEL OF DEATH** (Yid.: *Malekh ha-moves*)

The Jewish Angel of Death is traditionally depicted as being covered with thousands of eyes. The Angel stands at the head of the dying person with a drawn sword on the end of which clings a drop of bile. When the dying person sees the Angel, they are seized with convulsions and open their mouths at which point the bile drops, causing death.

In Shneour's version the Angel's blade is a *khalef*, a ritual slaughtering knife.

**ARBA-KANFES**

A ritual garment, worn under the shirts of observant male Jews, consisting of a rectangular fabric with a hole for the head and with tassels at each of the four corners.

**ELEL**

See *Jewish calendar*.

**GOT FUN AVROM**

The opening lines of a prayer recited by women and girls at the conclusion of *Shabbes*; one of the few traditional prayers composed in Yiddish rather than Hebrew.

**HAVDOLE** (Heb.: *Havdalah*)

Ceremony marking the end of *Shabbes* where blessings are made over wine.

## JEWISH CALENDAR

The narrator's diary follows the Jewish calendar and its entries span from the 20th of Elel (Heb. *Elul*) to the 23rd of Tishre (Heb. *Tishrei*)—approximately equivalent to the Gregorian Late August/September/Early October—a timeframe beginning toward the end of Elel, the month of introspection and repentance, and including the holidays of Rosh Hashanah (Jewish New Year), Yom Kippur, and Sukkes.

## KAPORE (Lit.: *atonement*)

A ritual on the eve of Yom Kippur that involves swinging a live chicken around one's head while reciting specific biblical passages. The chicken is then slaughtered and its meat usually donated to charity to be eaten as a pre–Yom Kippur meal.

## KHEYDER (often spelled "Cheder")

Traditional Jewish religious school for boys from around age five up to bar mitzvah. Study centers on learning Hebrew and the first five books of the Torah.

## LITHUANIA (Yid.: *Lite*)

Here, an area much larger than the modern state of Lithuania. Homeland of the Litvaks, a group whose regional identity is considerably older and more stable than the borders of Eastern Europe, living in the area roughly equivalent to modern-day Lithuania, Latvia, Belarus, and parts of northeast Poland. The Litvaks differed from the *Poylish* (Polish) Jews and *Galitsyaner* (Galician/Ukrainian) Jews in dialect, cuisine, and temperament.

## MAKHZER

Prayer book for the Jewish holidays.

## MAYREV (Heb.: *Maariv*)

Evening prayer service.

## MINYAN

A quorum of ten adult Jewish men, required for various religious obligations. Here the term refers to a gathering for prayers.

## MISHNA

The oldest part of the Talmud, containing the oral laws and traditions believed to have been passed down from Moses as a companion to the written Torah.

## MITZVAH (Yid.: *Mitsve*)

Good deed or commandment. While Gentiles are expected to follow the Ten Commandments, the Torah contains 613 commandments that an observant Jew must endeavor to follow.

## REB

Yiddish honorific, equivalent to "Mister." Used with full name, or first name only.

## SEGOL

Symbol used to indicate pronunciation of the vowel *e* in Hebrew, consisting of three dots arranged in a triangle. Shloyme compares it to the skulls he draws, the three dots representing the eye sockets and nasal cavity.

## SHABBES

The Jewish Sabbath, beginning at sundown on Friday evening and ending with *Havdole* on Saturday evening at dusk. Traditionally observant Jews are forbidden from all forms of work on *Shabbes*, including handling money, writing, traveling, or making fire.

## SHAMMES (*Shames*)

The caretaker of a synagogue. Often translated as "beadle" or "sexton."

## SHEL ROSH

*Tefillin* worn on the forehead.

## SHLIMAZL

A chronically unlucky person; a ne'er-do-well.

Shloyme, the Yiddish equivalent of Solomon, is the narrator's given name. Most of Shloyme's interactions in the city, even with his fellow Yiddish speakers, take place in Russian, the language those of his generation associated with secular learning and social prestige, and so to his acquaintances he is known as Salomon. While at home with his father the familiar diminutive form, Shloymke, is used (pronounced *Shleymke* in his native Litvak accent).

## SUKKES

Also known as the Feast of Tabernacles. An eight-day festival, beginning and ending with holy days. The festival is traditionally celebrated by building an outdoor hut, known as a *Sukkah*, the walls and roof of which are covered in *skhakh* (palm leaves or nearest available equivalent) where families eat their meals and sometimes sleep. The period in the middle of the festival, where work is permitted as normal, is known as *khalemoyd* (Heb.: *Chol Hamoed*).

## TEFILLIN (Yid.: *tfiln*)

Tefillin, often called phylacteries, are small leather boxes containing tiny scrolls of parchment, worn during morning prayer, on the forehead and arm, secured by leather straps.

## TISHRE

See *Jewish calendar*.

## TKHINES

Devotional texts and liturgy for women, usually in Yiddish, commonly printed in booklets.

## TREYF

Unkosher, impure, and forbidden according to Jewish dietary laws. The scene where Shloyme encounters hordes of unobservant Jews gleefully gorging themselves on *treyf* in Christian restaurants makes sense if we remember that on Yom Kippur—the holiest day of the year, when all observant Jews are busy fasting and praying—an apostate would be safe to break the rules without being seen (and if they were seen it would only be by others similarly profaning the holiday).

### YESHIVA (*yeshive*)

School focused on the study of religious texts, particularly the Talmud and Torah. *Yeshive bokherim* were adolescent boys who had shown enough intellectual promise to warrant further studies. Yeshivas were usually boarding schools, with students often having to leave home and travel some distance to study there. Meals for poorer students were often provided on a charitable basis by nearby families.

### YOM KIPPUR

The Day of Atonement, holiest day in the Jewish Year. Marked by a day of fasting, intensive prayer, and synagogue attendance.

Daniel Kennedy is a translator based in France. His forthcoming translations from the Yiddish include *Warsaw Stories* by Hersh Dovid Nomberg and *Tsilke the Wild* by Zusman Segalovitsh. He is the translation editor of *In geveb: A Journal of Yiddish Studies*.